MARC BROWN

ARTHUR, CLEAN YOUR ROOM!

Bottle Caps

Step into Reading® Sticker Books

Random House 🏠 New York

Copyright © 1999 by Marc Brown. All rights reserved under International and Pan-American Copyright Conventions. Published in the United States by Random House, Inc., New York, and simultaneously in Canada by Random House of Canada Limited, Toronto.

www.randomhouse.com/kids

Library of Congress Cataloging-in-Publication Data
Brown, Marc Tolon. Arthur, clean your room! / [text and illustrations by] Marc Brown. p. cm.
SUMMARY: His sister D.W. convinces Arthur to have a garage sale after his mother tells him to get rid of the junk in his room, but things do not work out exactly as he had planned.
ISBN 0-679-88467-X (trade) — ISBN 0-679-98467-4 (lib. bdg.)
[1. Aardvark—Fiction. 2. Orderliness—Fiction. 3. Garage sales—Fiction.
4. Brothers and sisters—Fiction.] I. Title. PZ7.B81618Ald 1999 [E]—dc21 98-43341
Printed in the United States of America 10 9 8 7 6 5 4 3 2 1

STEP INTO READING is a registered trademark of Random House, Inc.

ARTHUR® is a registered trademark of Marc Brown.

"Mom, I can't find
my Bionic 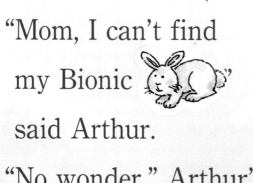"
said Arthur.

"No wonder," Arthur's mother said.

"Look at all this junk!"

"It's not junk," said Arthur.

"It IS junk," she said,

"and I want you to get rid of it—

NOW!"

"But how can I get rid of it?"
asked Arthur.
"Sell it," said D.W.
"You can make big "

"Have a  sale," said Mother.

"And have it today."

D.W. helped Arthur carry  of junk outside.

"I've always liked your Jolly Jingle Maker," said D.W. "Can I have it?"

"I'm selling it," said Arthur.

GARAGE SALE TODAY

ROCKS

Buster was the first 1 there.
"I can't believe you're selling
this Bionic Bunny Jet Fighter,"
said Buster. "I don't have a 💵
but I'll trade you my
Bionic 🐰 Spy 👓."

"Your Bionic Bunny Spy !"
said Arthur. "Okay, great trade!"
Buster ran to his
to get them.

Then Francine came along with
a  filled with comic books.
"My mom is making me get rid
of these," she said sadly.
"Oh, boy, Cool Cat comics!"
said Arthur.
"Wow!" said Francine.
"Is that a real
World Cup Soccer Game?"
"Almost new," said Arthur.
"I'll trade it for your comics."
"All right!" said Francine.

News spread, and Arthur's friends

all came with things to trade.

"Binky, that is so cool,"

said Arthur. "What is it?"

"My punching " said Binky.

"I want to trade it

for your  r Sam

"Good deal!" said Arthur.

Here are some stickers to use in *Arthur, Clean Your Room!* Each of these stickers matches one of the blue words in the story. Find each blue word and put the matching sticker on it.

My Own Arthur Story

by ....

Can you write and
illustrate a story about
Arthur's new garden?
Here are some stickers
to get you started.
Have fun!

Muffy showed up next.

"You've always liked

my clubhouse

she said. "Want to trade?"

"Sure," said Arthur.

"Is this cute

really yours, Arthur?"

she giggled.

"It's yours now," he said.

"It's never been worn."

The Brain came with a
"It needs a little work," he said.

"I'll trade you my
said Sue Ellen.

Prunella traded
her  poster.

Fern had a t  r
that Arthur really liked.

Arthur was happy.

His old stuff was gone.

D.W. ran to the

"You didn't sell your

Jolly Jingle Maker," she said.

"But I got rid of all my other

old stuff," said Arthur.

"I'll count your money,"

said D.W.

"Well," he said,

"I didn't really get any . . ."

"But I got all this great new stuff,"
said Arthur.

"If Mom sees this," said D.W.,

"you are in big trouble."

"You're right," he said,

"but what am I going to do?"

"I have a plan,"

whispered D.W.

Later that day, Arthur's mother
went to check his room.
Arthur followed her up the st
He crossed his f
and held his breath.

"Good job, Arthur," she said.

"You got rid of all your junk."

Just then they heard a big

CRASH!

They ran to D.W.'s room.

Junk was everywhere.

"Dora Winifred!" shouted Mother.

"What is this mess?"

"It's not a mess," said D.W.

"It's business.

Arthur is paying me rent.

And he owes me a

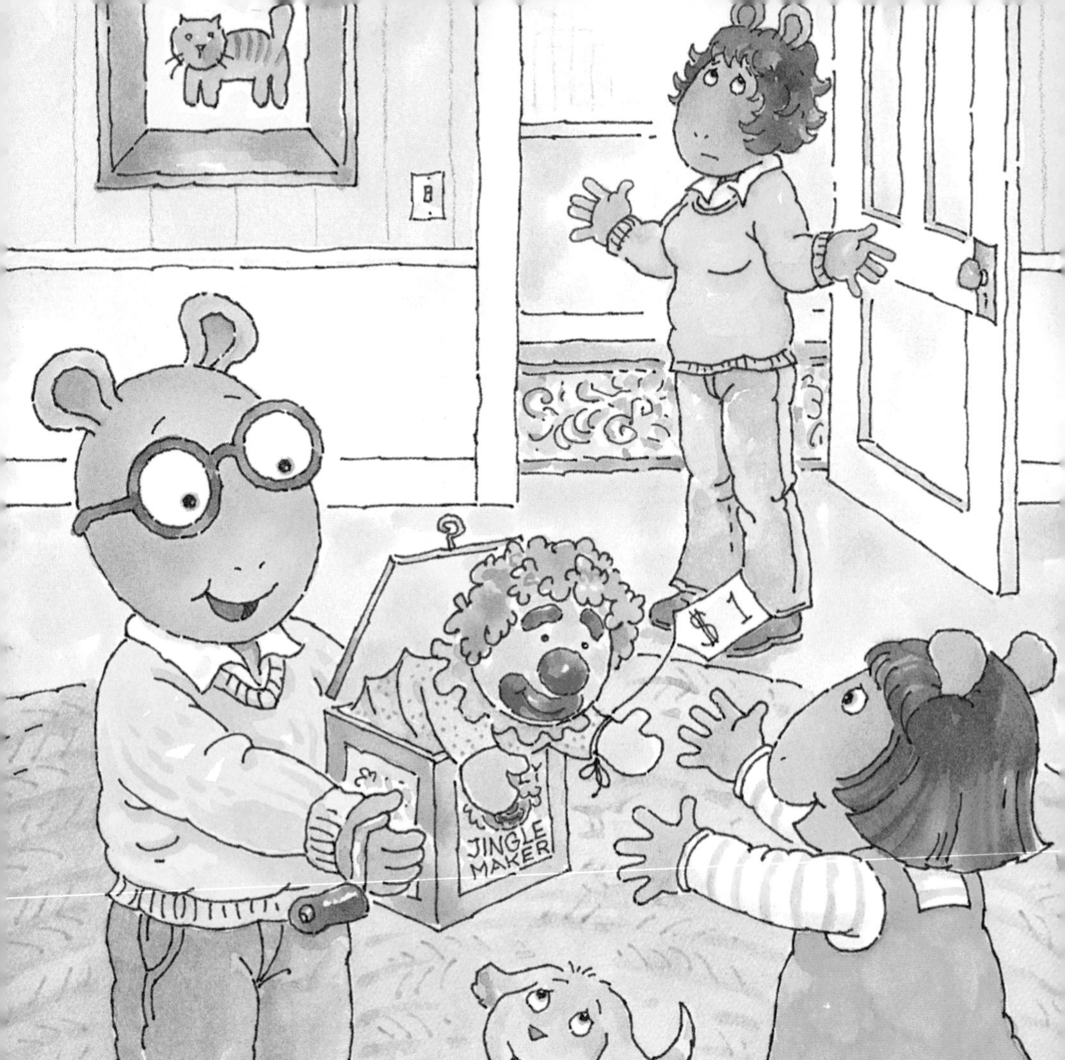

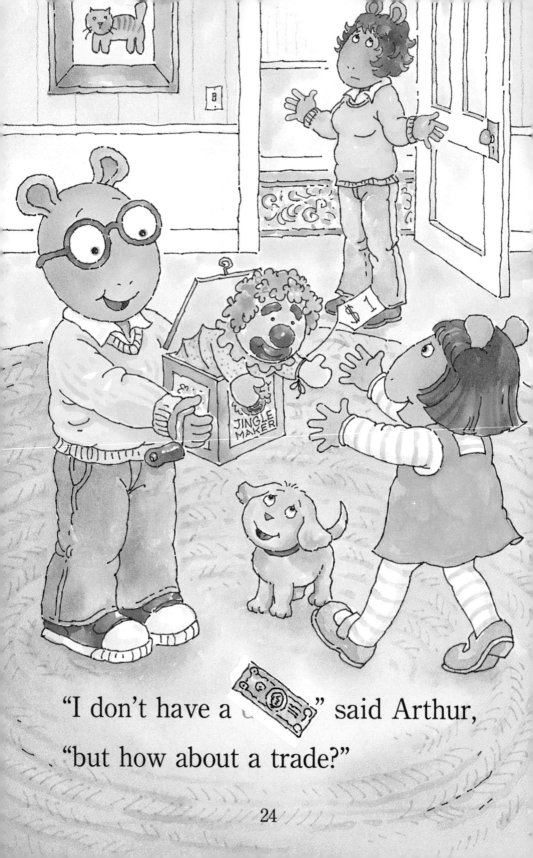

"I don't have a 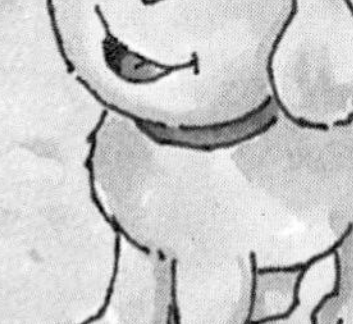," said Arthur,
"but how about a trade?"

PEAN

THE ART OF

CHARLES

b.

NUTS®

...SCHULZ

Edited and designed by Chip Kidd

PANTHEON BOOKS   NEW YORK   2001

WITH AN INTRODUCTION BY JEAN SCHULZ

AND COMMENTARY BY CHIP KIDD

PHOTOGRAPHS BY GEOFF SPEAR

ORIGINAL ART FROM THE COLLECTIONS OF JEAN, CRAIG, AND MONTE SCHULZ
ARCHIVAL *PEANUTS* STRIPS FROM THE COLLECTIONS OF CHRIS WARE AND CHIP KIDD

PRODUCTION ASSISTANCE BY JOHN KURAMOTO

"Goodbys always make my throat hurt . . . I need more hellos . . ."
—*Charlie Brown, 1967*

In July of 2000, at the invitation of the executors of Charles Schulz's estate, the photographer Geoff Spear and I were granted unlimited access to the *Peanuts* archive and the collections of the Schulz family in Santa Rosa, California, where we photographed for two weeks. Shortly thereafter, the cartoonist Chris Ware lent me his extensive collection of vintage *Peanuts* strips, many of them dating from the first three years of its existence, 1950-1953.

This book is the result, and it attempts to present the work of Charles M. Schulz in the way I felt it should be seen. And, to be honest, it's also a way I can avoid saying goodbye to it. To them.

For all of us who ate our school lunches alone and didn't have any hope of sitting anywhere near the little red-haired girl and never got any valentines and struck out every single time we were shoved to the plate for Little League, we had *Peanuts* and Charlie Brown to help take the sting out of it.

I find when you look closer than you're supposed to at something you think you're familiar with, you're introduced to it all over again.

And you say hello.

—Chip Kidd

INTRODUCTION

Sparky was a genius.

That is the answer to the unanswerable questions of "why" and "how." I recognized it when I first knew him, I spent the next 25 years asking the same things others ask, and always came back to the same answer. The essence of his genius is: We can't know it, quantify it, explain it; we can, simply, enjoy it. If those of us who are part of his circle puzzle over the questions and struggle for answers, no one struggled more than Sparky himself.

He understood intuitively things he couldn't explain. Things he couldn't even put into words. He could go only so far as to answer the perennial question "Where do your ideas come from?"

The ideas Sparky used are out there in the world. We all know them and that is why we relate to them. It is the particular twist Sparky put to the ideas that described his genius, and that draws us, enchanted, into his frame.

I believe there are people of genius around us, but few are fortunate enough to have their genius match the moment. A thousand years ago, Sparky would have been a storyteller, the person in the tribe or the clan who collected the tribal lore and repeated it for each generation. He understood instinctively the value of the story which illustrates a human truth, and which allows his listeners to take from it what they need at the time. The best stories can be told over and over again—forever new—because the listener changes.

Sparky loved his *Big-Little Books* when he was small, when he was in high school he escaped into the world of Sherlock Holmes, and always he loved adventure comics. He actually wanted to draw an adventure strip, but it was the wistful, innocent way he illustrated an emotion, expressed through the eyes of a small person, that caught the attention of the comics editors. And so it was children he drew on for his cartoons.

Children, he would have told you, are simply adults "with the lids still on." He believed firmly that we are the product of our genes and that all of the characteristics are there within us as children, simmering, waiting to emerge. So the envy and anger expressed in "Good Ol' Charlie Brown. How I hate him" in the first strip, shocks us, but Sparky knew, whether or not we want to admit it, children feel that emotion. When Sparky saw a child with a very strong personality, he observed how difficult that person would be "when the lid comes off."

Sparky loved to sit in his ice arena over lunch and have an interesting and varied group around, and he was very good in front of an audience. He knew how to draw his story out to hold people's attention. His directness enlivened any conversation and he probed others with questions. In these situations he was like the storyteller of old—interacting with his audience in a very intimate way.

But the comic strip is a long way from the storyteller of a thousand years ago. The cartoonist puts his drawings and words on paper and it is weeks before his audience sees them. Immediacy and personality must be elucidated in a different way. The comic strip storyteller of 20th century America has to tell a story that stretches across 3000 miles, and draw scenes of snow pranks that make people laugh in Hawaii as well as in Vermont or Michigan.

Like the novelist, the cartoonist must go into himself or herself, and draw upon what is there. It is a solitary craft.

Sparky frequently wasn't sure if something he'd drawn was funny. Certainly he'd receive feedback, but it would be months later. The spontaneity was missing. Often I'd stop at his studio and look over a stack of dailies on his desk. When I laughed out loud, or told him how funny I thought they were, he was truly grateful. "Oh, I'm so glad you think it's funny. I'm never sure," he'd say. He loved people's positive responses, and at the same time, he had to shut out the voices. He had to draw what *he* thought was funny and *hope* that his audience liked it too. He was always glad to know people liked his characters or a particular storyline, but he knew he couldn't write to that audience; he always wrote for himself.

He began quite early in his career to use biblical references. Occasionally, someone would write to say, "How dare you use religious material in a comic strip?" His response was that as long as he had used the reference with integrity, he was satisfied that he was on firm ground. On the other hand, once in the 70s, he used a take-off on the title *I Heard the Owl Call My Name*. He got a letter saying this was a sacred phrase in a Native American tribe. Sparky wrote an apology. He admitted he hadn't realized that he was overstepping propriety.

Sparky sometimes tried out an idea on me or others. For example he'd say, "How would it be if Charlie Brown goes to camp and meets this other kid who won't say anything except 'Shut up and leave me alone.'?" Well, it's difficult to imagine that as a funny storyline, but I knew better than to say no, and of course, because of the funny drawing and the particular way he paced the strip and the story, it became a funny sequence. If this or any new character made for a good storyline, Sparky might go back and resurrect the character a year later for a second camp episode, but more often than not, that first appearance would be the last. He explained that the character was too one-dimensional to create opportunities for humor.

In order to produce a strip every day, he had to rely on characters whose personalities themselves engendered ideas. Sparky always had a pen handy to write down any notions that came to him, or if we were in the car he'd ask me to write for him. Frequently, at the symphony, I'd see him reach into his pocket for his pad and pencil. On the way home he'd tell me the idea he had—but what he related to me at the time was only the germ of what would become a fully realized daily or Sunday page. He could come up with ideas from almost any situation because his characters had such distinct personalitites and idiosyncrasies.

As much as most of us are drawn to the personalities and the situations and the lines the characters deliver, Sparky was always quick to point out that the appeal of *Peanuts* is still funny drawing. He would use a yellow lined pad to "doodle," drawing the characters in antic poses, rolling over, flying upside down, etc. These provided him with ideas.

When the strip ended, the response was overwhelming. Sparky touched people deeply and often changed their lives, as the thousands of letters attested:

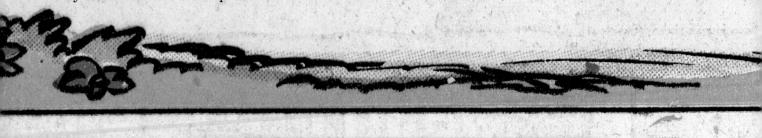

"I remember [as a child] often being consumed by feelings of profound anxiety and unrest, and yet as soon as I could come home to read my Peanuts books, I was peaceful, even happy."

"When I was about 11 years old I had to go into the hospital and I was very scared. My mother had to leave me after visiting hours, but my stuffed Snoopy didn't. I held it all night long."

"I often identified with Charlie Brown's feelings of inadequacy, of not fitting in anywhere. And my favorite character was always Linus, who was sensible but had an almost magical sense of the power of his innocence and imagination."

"Charlie Brown and the gang were a solace and a balm to my soul. I always wanted to tell this to Mr. Schulz. So now I tell you."

Sparky once said, "I would be satisfied if they wrote on my tombstone 'He made people happy.'"

He did that, and so much more.

— JEAN SCHULZ

Library of Congress Cataloging-in-Publication Data: Schulz, Charles M.
Peanuts : the art of Charles M. Schulz.
ISBN 0-375-71463-4
1. Schulz, Charles M.--Peanuts. I. Title.
PN6728.P4 S3262 2001   741.5'973--dc21   2001021577

www.pantheonbooks.com • BOOK DESIGN BY CHIP KIDD
Printed in China • First Paperback Edition
2 4 6 8 9 7 5 3

PEANUTS
NOW WHO DREW THAT?
CHARLIE BROWN
WHAT AN INSULT! THAT'S

…chulz's drawing tools, photographed July 2000. The tray is as it was left the previous December, when he had finished …s last strip. It sat vertically along the right side of his drawing table. Note the Snoopy bandage.

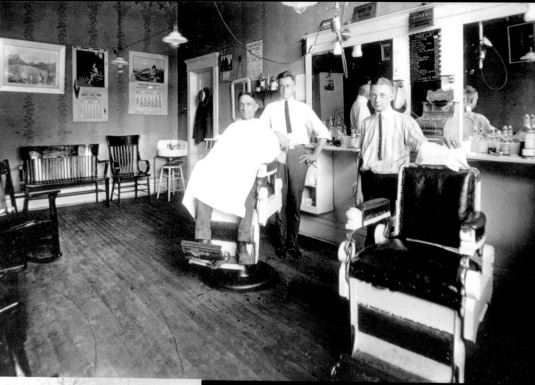

Upper left: Dena and Carl Schulz, 1920

Above: Carl (at left) in his barbershop with Monroe Halverson

Far left: Sparky as a young boy, 1927

Left: A boy, his dad, his dog and his sled. Winter in Minnesota, 1926

Right and lower left: Sparky and Spike—a pointer, not a beagle, 1935

Below, center: Sparky offers Spike a drink, early 1940s

Lower right: Sparky, Dena and Carl, taken shortly before Sparky's February 1943 departure for Fort Snelling, in Minneapolis

J. S. Com.; "Times Revue."

Edward Schmidt—Thumb Tacks; German Club; Treas., Vice-Pres. International Club; Class Com.; "Cehisean"; Commence. Com.

If Sparky (nicknamed for the horse "Sparkplug" from the comic strip *Barney Google*) doesn't look too happy in his high school yearbook photo, that's because he wasn't. And if he looks a little young to be graduating, that's because he is—after first grade he was "promoted" two grades ahead and Charlie Brown was effectively born. "I was the smallest, the youngest, the shyest. I managed to flunk at least one subject a year."

Idelle Schnitzer—Girls' League; G. A. A.

Dorothy Schroeder—Girls' League; Girl Reserve; Treas. Triads; Vice-Pres. Masque and Foil; Ex. Bd. G. A. A.; "C" Club; All-City Letter; Referee; Commence. Com.; Honor Roll.

Charles Schulz—"Cehisean." But he did love to draw. On the opposite page is an exercise from his high school art class. The teacher, Minette Paro, asked the students to draw small objects in groups of threes. "They were spectacular because they were things you wouldn't even think of," Miss Paro recalled. "That means that his mind was working every minute. He isn't worried about what's going on the paper, it's in his mind, it's got to come out."

Howard Schultz—Dramatic Club; Bowling Club; Pres., Sec. Mid. Hi-Y; Assemblies; Student Council; Baseball; Capt. Basketball; "C" Club; National Honor Society.

Beverlie Schuneman.

Marjorie Searing—Ski Club; Table Tennis Club; Girls' League; "Times"; Honor Roll; Quill and Scroll.

Note: Little could Schulz have known that in less than ten years he'd be in Hitler's Germany while Dachau was being liberated.

Hyam Segell—Stamp Club; International Club; Pres. Latin Club; Vice-Pres. Chess Club; Pres. Debating Club; Chr. Class Com.; Assemblies; "Cehisean"; Commence. Com.; Honor Roll; National Honor Society.

Don Shannon—Aeronautics Club; Pres. Ski Club; Orchestra; Chr. Class Com.; "Cehisean."

Lois Shirley—Girls' League; Girl Reserve; Masque and Foil; Ski Club; Gym Demonstration; "Cehisean."

In an unfortunately symbolic turn of events, his drawings for this yearbook were accepted by the editors, and then, unbeknownst to him, unceremoniously dropped. He found out only when the book was released.

Stanley Simon—Table Tennis Club; Chess Club; Stamp Club; "C" Club; International Club; Class Com.; "Cehisean"; Tennis; I. M. Basketball; Commence. Com.; Honor Roll.

Mavajean Simpson—Girl Reserve; Dramatic Club; Treas. Literary Club; Girls' League; J. S. Com.; Class Com.; Band Concert; Gym Demonstration;
"World"; Assemblies; "Times"; Commence. Com.

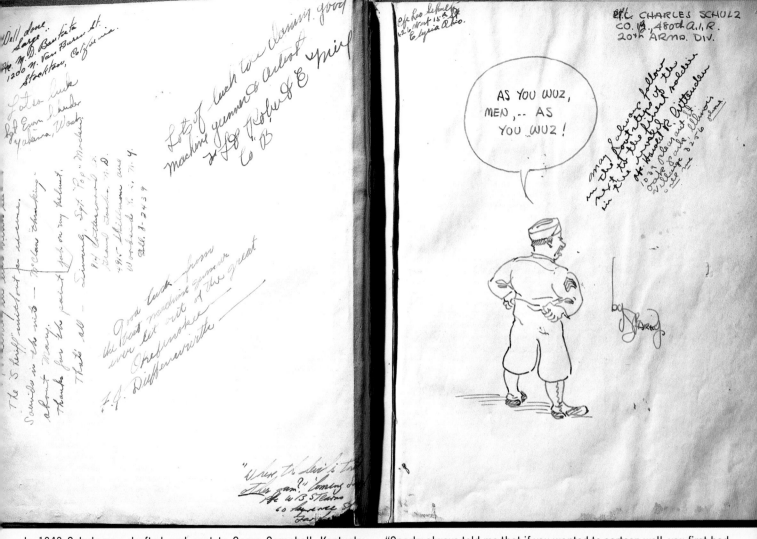

In 1943 Schulz was drafted and sent to Camp Campbell, Kentucky, where he spent the next two years, eventually shipping out to Germany. Though a true patriot, he hated the realities of military life and kept a sketchbook, called "As We Were," in order help pass the time. The drawings vary between being realistic and "cartoony."

"Sparky always told me that if you wanted to cartoon well, you first had to be able to draw things in a realistic manner," said Paige Braddock, a senior vice president at Schulz's Creative Associates and a cartoonist in her own right. "He didn't feel realism and cartooning were mutually exclusive, but rather integrated in the final caricature."

MAIL CALL!!
1.
CHOW!!
2.
11:30!! P.X. IS OPEN!
3.
BUT..
"B" COMPANY OUTSIDE FOR POLICE-UP!!
4.
5.
THEY CAN HARDLY MAKE IT.

Enlisted Men's Barracks and Mess Halls, Camp Campbell, Ky.–Tenn.

"ARMY ADDRESSES"

POST CARD

PLACE
ONE CENT
STAMP
HERE

GENUINE CURTEICH — CHICAGO "C.T. ART COLORTONE (R.U.S.)

DISTRIBUTED BY NEETS NEWS ADV. CI. TN.

From
Cpl. Charlie Shutz
37750437
Co. B, 8th A. D. Bn.
A. P. O. 444
20th Arm'd. Div.
Camp Campbell, Ky.,
U. S. Army.
So long,
"Charlie"

Miss Gene Gray
36½ 8th Ave. So.,
Centertown,
Kansas

Art Instruction Inc.

Back from the war in 1945, Schulz took a job as instructor at his alma mater in St. Paul, Art Instruction Inc. Here he met the man who would become his mentor, Frank Wing, creator of the depression-era strip *Yesterdays*.

Wing and Sparky forged a lifelong friendship, though the older cartoonist was wary of the young upstart's "modernist" style of draftsmanship.

HERE ARE THE **ARTISTS** WHO WILL INSTRUCT YOU:

This drawing, from 1950, looks worthy of *The New Yorker*, but Schulz didn't think so—he never submitted any of his work to the venerable weekly, "because it was hopeless."

" Waiter, there's a hare in this soup ! "

But he did send drawings to other periodicals. *Timeless Topix*, a Roman Catholic comics publication, hired him in 1945 to do freelance lettering and published his very first comic strip, a one-shot called *Just Keep Laughing*. His first serial cartoon series saw print in 1947 when the *St. Paul Pioneer Press* agreed to publish *Sparky's Li'l Folks*, which soon became simply *Li'l Folks*. It ran for two years in the women's section. The following eleven pages are taken from his personal scrapbook of these strips, many seen here for the first time since their original publication.

This page features some undated sketches, probably from the early 1950s. Note here the prototype for Snoopy, whose ears have a life of their own.

Just Keep Laughing..

By Spanky

"THE NEW LARGE ECONOMY SIZE HAS CERTAINLY BEEN A HELP TO THE HOUSING SHORTAGE."

"HAPPY BIRTHDAY, MOM, AND IF YOU DON'T LIKE IT, THE MAN SAID I COULD EXCHANGE IT FOR A HOCKEY PUCK!"

"AND THIS IS MISS FOLSOM, OUR NEW INSTRUCTOR IN ANCIENT HISTORY."

"Y'KNOW, JUDY, I THINK I COULD LEARN TO LOVE YOU IF YOUR BATTING AVERAGE WAS JUST LITTLE HIGHER"

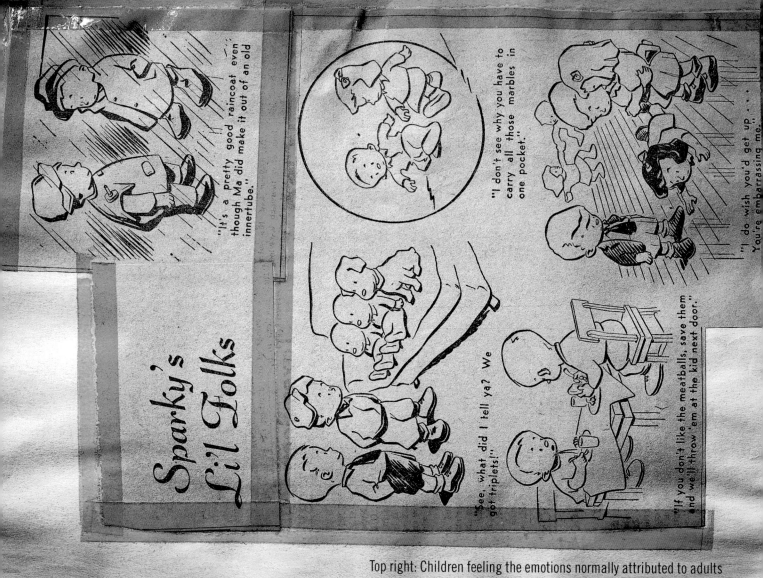

Top right: Children feeling the emotions normally attributed to adults started in *Li'l Folks* and became a staple of Schulz's work throughout his career.

Li'l Folks
BY SPARKY

"You moved!"

"Happy birthday to you . . .
"Happy birthday to you . . .
"Happy birthday, dear . . .
"What did you say your name was?"

"Y'know, if you were sure that you and I were going to the same high school, I'd ask you to the senior prom."

"No, no, no! . . . You don't seem to understand!"

It's not Beethoven, but it was a sign of things to come.

The "dog as rebel" theme appeared as early as 1947.

Li'l Folks

BY SPARKY

"I DREAD THE DAY WHEN I HAVE TO MEET BEETHOVEN FACE TO FACE."

"BROWN? WHY, NO..... WHAT MAKES YOU THINK I'VE SEEN CHARLIE BROWN?"

The seeds of *Peanuts* are planted all over this cartoon from 1949, as Charlie Brown sees print for the fourth time (buried in sand), a very Snoopy-like pup is a head-rest and head-starter, and Beethoven makes a cameo during Schroeder's pre-piano phase.

Our cap-clutching li'l friend uses a line that Schroeder will paraphrase more than a decade later (note the typo), when he describes his feelings about Lucy.

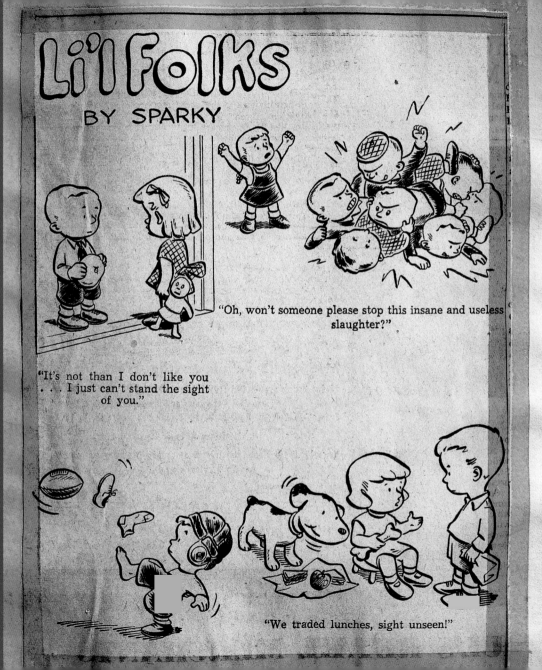

The playful use of scale in *Li'l Folks* puts small children into a world that's often too big or too small for them, an idea that would be continued in *Peanuts*—first physically and then emotionally.

"LET'S GET OUT OF HERE...THIS GIVES ME THE CHILLS!"

This gag, from the late 1940s, seems eerily to predict the government's impending crackdown in the mid-1950s on comic books deemed "too intense" for young children. Though the titles Schulz chose seem gratuitous, they're remarkably similar to what was being published at the time.

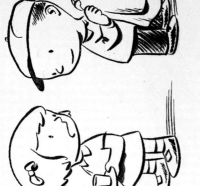

Li'l Folks
BY SPARKY

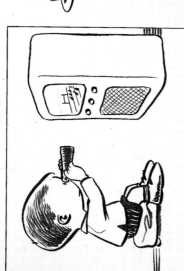

" JUST HANG YOUR COAT ANYWHERE, AND MAKE YOURSELF TO HOME."

" TRY TO BE MORE PATIENT...WEINERS DON'T ROAST IN A SECOND, YOU KNOW!"

At left is the original art for the strip above, from the late 1940s. Schulz was ever mindful of the loss of line quality that a drawing suffered on its way to newsprint, and his minimal, simplified style was easily able to withstand a possible increase in line thickness in the final printed version.

"OH, BOY LOOKIT ME . . . I HAS FOUND A LITTLE DOGGIE!"

In May of 1948, Schulz got his first big break.

"Although I realized it was against all rules of professionalism, I sent a finished drawing to *The Saturday Evening Post*. [Submissions to such magazines were usually done in rough form and sent in batches of ten to fifteen.] Several days later I received a note in the mail that said 'Check Tuesday for spot drawing of boy on lounge.' I was so used to having my work rejected I thought the note meant that I should check my mailbox on Tuesday, that they were going to send the drawing back. A couple of hours later I figured it out and, of course, was ecstatic. This was my first sale to a major market."

Between 1948 and 1950, he eventually sold seventeen cartoons to editor John Bailey. He was paid forty dollars apiece.

"I tried all sorts of different things, and could never sell anything, and it was the breakthrough to *The Saturday Evening Post* with the style, then, that I was working on . . . Little kids with great big heads saying things that were a little bit out of context."

At right is an idea that would eventually be "recycled" into a future *Peanuts* strip.

THE SATURDAY EVENING POST   SCHULZ

Schulz would use a yellow legal pad to script and rough the strip. He'd then do the lettering first, before the art, inking it in with this C-5 pen tip. Once he was satisfied with the text, then he'd draw the finished art.

"PEDIGREE" PENS

William Mitchell

ESTABLISHED 1825

"PEDIGREE"
REGISTERED TRADE MARK

ROUND HAND PENS

FOR FORMAL WRITING

LEFT OBLIQUE
No. 3
1 DOZEN
WITH RESERVOIRS

WILLIAM MITCHELL
BIRMINGHAM & LONDON

R. Esterbrook & Co.

PENS

1858

Made in U.S.A.

914 RADIO

144-Pens

He didn't pencil everything in first, as most cartoonists do. "I pencil as little as possible," Schulz said in 1997. "Just enough to get the heights and the space right. But I draw the faces with the pen when I'm doing it. Because you want that spontaneity, you don't want to be just following the pencil line."

He used a 914 Radio, and relied on these pen nibs so much that when the company announced it was going out of business, he bought the entire remaining stock. The hundreds of boxes saw him through the rest of his career.

This two-layer drawing, on construction paper, was done in 1950 as part of a proposal for a magazine to be called *Divertimento*, organized by Schulz's friend from Art Instruction Bill Ryan. The project never left this developmental stage.

The top orange layer has die-cut windows, behind which sits a pre-Charlie Brown round-headed figure. When the page was turned, it revealed the image below with its visual "trick" of the flowers as paintings.

THESE ARE GOOD STRIPS, MR. SASSEVILLE, BUT WE HERE AT UNITED FEATURES ARE INTERESTED IN A DIFFERENT TYPE CHARACTER!

In the spring of 1950, Schulz collected his best strips from *The Saturday Evening Post* and *The St. Paul Pioneer Press* and sent them to United Feature Syndicate in New York City. After more than six weeks with no response, he wrote them asking if his package had been lost.

Soon after, he received a letter saying not only had they gotten the package, but they wanted him to come to Manhattan and meet about publication. He did, and on October 2, 1950 **Peanuts** was born.

It's no secret he wasn't fond of the name, thrust upon him by United Feature. He wanted to call it 'Good Ol' Charlie Brown,' but the syndicate was wary of focusing attention on just one character and wanted something that suggested a whole 'cast.' Sparky was so thrilled to be syndicated he accepted their mandate.

Above: This gag (probably from 1950) refers to Sparky's friend from Art Instruction Jim Sasseville, and is a goof on the shape of Charlie Brown's head. Sasseville's style was more representational.

10/2
SCHULZ 1951

Schulz pays homage to one of his heroes, George Herriman (creator of *Krazy Kat*), in this witty drawing of Ignatz beaning Charlie Brown, from 1952. He couldn't have known how prophetic this image is: the passing of the torch from one genius of the the form to the next.

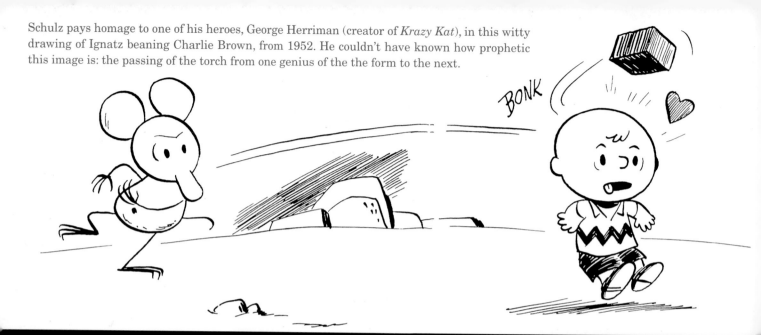

BONK

PEANUTS BEGINS

The four-panel nature of *Peanuts* freed Schulz from the group-montage format of *Li'l Folks*, a change that allowed him to grow as a draftsman and storyteller. Instead of one-liner, single-panel gags, he could now develop situations for the characters that went from point a to b, then c, and d. But this could prove restrictive as well—the syndicate limited the format to *exactly* four panels of equal size , so it could be run vertically, horizontally, or in stacked blocks of two. Decades passed before Schulz was able to pull rank and construct the panels as he saw fit, even occasionally going back to a single panel.

It's hard to imagine how different *Peanuts* was from its contemporaries when it started, because so much of what made it unique—its graphic simplicity, its poetic yet embittered and alienated sense of humor—has been so widely copied since. Schulz maintained that the strip was anything but an instant hit and took years to develop an audience.

Seeing *Peanuts* from the very beginning is fascinating in light of what it would become. The roots of the iconic characters are there, but they have a long way to go. Knowing how they will evolve makes their debuts all the more intriguing, like seeing baby pictures of celebrities.

"PEANUTS"

Snoopy did not "think," at first, at least not in words.

Charlie Brown was probably turned into a cyclops in this panel by a printer who thought his left eye was a speck of dirt on the plate and had it removed—it happened more than once (see opposite, lower left panel). Such was the initial confusion brought on by the minimal style of the strip.

YOU'RE GLAD TO SEE ME, HUH, SNOOPY?

BOY, WHAT A GREETING!

THIS TOUCHES ME DEEPLY...

NEVER BEFORE IN ALL MY LIFE HAS ANYONE MADE ME FEEL SO WELCOME! *SNIFF* *SNIFF*

Only seven newspapers picked up the strip from the very beginning:

The Washington Post

The Chicago Tribune

Star Tribune of Minneapolis

The Morning Call, (Allentown, Pa.)

Bethlehem Globe-Times

The Denver Post

The Seattle Times

By 2000, the total was over 2,500.

SNOOPY WON'T BE ABLE TO GET INTO THAT DOGHOUSE! IT'S TOO SMALL!!

HOW COULD YOU MAKE A MISTAKE LIKE THAT? WHAT KIND OF A CARPENTER ARE YOU?

THIS IS NOT A DOGHOUSE... THIS IS A BIRDHOUSE!

OH...

CHOMP! CHOMP! CHOMP!

POW!

The first color Sunday strips appeared in 1952. Like the dailies, they were designed so they could be run several different ways, to accommodate varying formats of a host of newspapers. Sunday strips could run with just the bottom six panels by themselves, or with the accompanying top "title" panel. The top right panel was designed to be strictly optional—if there was space for it, fine. If not, it could be dropped without any significant loss to the storyline.

"PEANUTS"

HEY, CHARLIE BROWN!

GEE, WITH SHIRTS JUST ALIKE IT'S HARD TO TELL YOU TWO APART!

ALL RIGHT, DON'T LOOK SO INSULTED!!

4/12 SCHULZ

"PEANUTS"

LET'S SEE NOW... A FEW GRAINS OF SALT.... ONE TEASPOON VANILLA....

TWO CUPS OF LIGHT CREAM... TWO EGGS SEPARATED...

RATS! IT'S JUST NO USE!!

NO MATTER WHAT YOU DO TO IT...A MUD PIE IS STILL A MUD PIE!

4/13 SCHULZ

"PEANUTS"

POOR SCHROEDER... HE THOUGHT HE WAS GOING TO WIN AN AMATEUR CONTEST

HE PLAYED ALL FORTY-EIGHT PRELUDES AND FUGUES FROM BACH'S " WELL-TEMPERED CLAVIER "!

AND HE DIDN'T WIN?!

HE DIDN'T EVEN COME CLOSE...

SOMEONE ELSE CAME ON, AND PLAYED THE ACCORDION REAL FAST!

7/25 SCHULZ

"PEANUTS" — I WOULDN'T WANT TO MARRY A REAL YOUNG MAN

"PEANUTS" — SPRING IS COMING, CHARLIE BROWN... / HE IS?

"PEANUTS" — SAY! I THINK I DO!

OF COURSE NOT, BUT YOU ALSO SHOULDN'T MARRY ONE WHO IS TOO OLD

NOT "HE" IS... "IT" IS! / "IT" IS WHAT? / IT IS COMING!

NO, I GUESS I DON'T

HOW ABOUT TWENTY-THREE? / I THINK THAT'S TOO OLD...

WHAT IS COMING? / SPRING IS COMING!! / HE IS?

IT TURNED OUT TO BE ONLY DIRT...

WHEN MEN GET TO BE THAT AGE, THEY'RE USUALLY PRETTY SET IN THEIR WAYS!

SOMEDAY I'LL PROBABLY DRIVE THIS POOR GIRL CRAZY!

BUT FOR ONE BRIEF, EXCITING MOMENT I THOUGHT I NEEDED A SHAVE!

PEANUTS by CHARLES M. SCHULZ

Tm. Reg. U. S. Pat. Off.—All rights reserved
Copr. 1952 by United Feature Syndicate, Inc.

3-30

Lucy first appeared in 1952 as a saucer-eyed baby, and a sweet-natured one at that.
Charlie Brown was often her baby-sitter and counselor in the early years. It didn't last long.

Above: Lucy demonstrates an athletic skill in 1953 that would vanish in later years, when her baseball prowess would consist of watching in wonderment as fly balls drop at her feet or soar over her head.

Left: Schroeder's status as prodigy only goes so far.

Right: Charlie Brown's stint as William Tell has safety in mind.

Bottom: No good deed goes unpunished, as a typical Schulz punchline renders a lot of fraught anxiety ultimately misspent.

DID YOU LOSE AGAIN TODAY, CHARLIE BROWN?

YEAH,...EIGHTY-THREE TO TWELVE...

THEY GOT ALL THE BREAKS!

♪?

KIND OF WARM OUT TODAY FOR EAR MUFFS, ISN'T IT?

WHY DO I HAVE TO SUFFER SUCH INDIGNITIES!?

Snoopy thinks a thought with words for the first time, 1951.
See opposite for the first time in color.

YOU REALIZE THAT THE SCORE IS SIXTY TO NOTHING, DON'T YOU?

UH, HUH

WELL, DON'T WORRY ABOUT IT...WE'LL GET 'EM BACK IN THE SECOND INNING!

"PEANUTS"

"A" IS FOR APPLE

PEANUTS

By Schulz

C'MON, SNOOPY!

YIPPEE!

THAT'S MY BOY!

SAY....IT'S GETTING LATE...

I'VE GOT TO BE GOING HOME

ME, TOO

I DIDN'T REALIZE IT WAS SO LATE

?

THERE THEY GO... LEAVING ME ALONE AGAIN! DO ANY OF THEM EVER INVITE ME OVER TO SPEND THE NIGHT? NO!

ALL I'M GOOD FOR IS A FEW LAUGHS!

RATS!

THEY'RE WILLING TO HAVE ME ENTERTAIN THEM DURING THE DAY, BUT AS SOON AS IT STARTS GETTING DARK, THEY ALL GO OFF, AND LEAVE ME!

WELL, I'LL SHOW 'EM!.... I DON'T NEED THEIR COMPANY!

I CAN ALWAYS SIT HOME, AND WATCH TELEVISION!

SNOOPY

"PEANUTS"

YOU LOOK SO COMFORTABLE, CHARLIE BROWN...

LET ME TAKE YOUR SHOES OFF FOR YOU SO YOU'LL BE EVEN MORE COMFORTABLE

By Schulz

IT SNOWED ST NIGHT, HARLIE BROWN!

WHY DON'T YOU GO DOWN IN THE BASEMENT, GET YOUR SLED, AND MAKE THE FIRST SLIDE OF THE WINTER?

HMM

I'LL DO IT! I'LL BE THE FIRST ONE!!

OPEN THE DOOR!

ED!!

SCREECH!!

SOMETIMES I GET THE BEST OF THAT OL' CHARLIE BROWN!

26

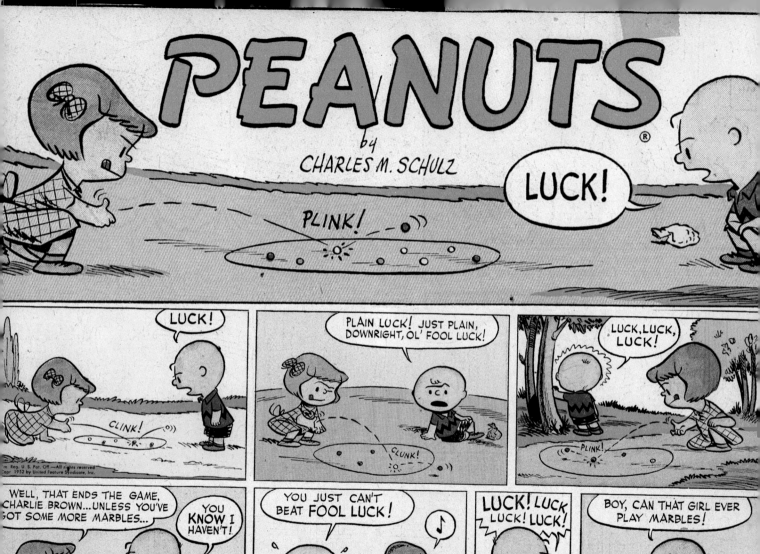

"PEANUTS"

HE'LL KICK MY HAND! I JUST KNOW HE WILL!

Charlie Brown's first failed football kick was at the hands of Violet, not Lucy—on November 14, 1951.

Where Lucy will be motivated by malice, Violet is just scared that she will be kicked by mistake, and balks at the last minute, leaving Charlie Brown to a fate that Lucy was to hand him throughout the duration of the strip.

"PEANUTS"

A PARTY? WHY, YES, I THINK I CAN COME...

"PEANUTS"

I THINK I'LL ENTER THAT CONTEST!

I CAN'T GO THROUGH WITH IT!

Copr. 1951 by United Feature Syndicate, Inc.

WHO ELSE IS GOING TO BE THERE?

ALL YOU HAVE TO DO IS COMPLETE THE SENTENCE IN FIFTY WORDS OR LESS

Copr. 1951 by United Feature Syndicate, Inc.

?

WILL YOU BE SERVING ICE CREAM?

Copr. 1951 by United Feature Syndicate, Inc.

OF COURSE, WITH ME IT'S GOING TO HAVE TO BE "LESS"...

11-12

SCHULZ

YOU DIDN'T KICK THE BALL, CHARLIE BROWN... WHY DIDN'T YOU KICK IT?

11-14 SCHULZ

SHE HUNG UP!

11-12 SCHULZ

I DON'T KNOW FIFTY WORDS!

"One of the main things to avoid is thinking too far ahead of yourself. Try to think of your daily episodes without concentrating too heavily on the overall theme of your comic feature. While you are concentrating on these daily episodes, trying to get the most humorous idea you can out of each, you will also be developing the personalities of your characters. You will find that ideas will begin to come from these personalities.

"As your ideas develop personalities and as your personalities develop more ideas, the overall theme of your feature will then begin to take form. This really is the only practical way to develop a good solid comic-strip feature."

—Charles Schulz, from *Developing a Comic Strip*, 1959

PEANUTS

by

CHARLES M. SCHULZ

I WONDER IF IT'S NICE OUTSIDE TODAY...

I'LL BE GLAD WHEN I LEARN TO GET OUT OF BED LIKE OTHER PEOPLE!

KLUNK!

LUCY

OH, MY!

HERE COMES CHARLIE BROWN, AND I'M STILL IN MY SLEEPIES!

WHAT'S HE DOING HERE SO EARLY?

A GIRL CAN'T TALK TO A FELLOW WHILE SHE'S STILL IN HER SLEEPIES!

I'LL HAVE TO HIDE IN MY ROOM

LUCY! WHERE ARE YOU?

OH, NO! HE'S COMING RIGHT IN HERE...

?

HI!

5-25

SCHUL

"The humor that I introduced in 1950 was a very concise sort of humor. It grew out of magazine cartooning. I drew very brief incidents in the first *Peanuts* strips. Then as it began to grow and the characters developed, more conversation entered into it, and the characters themselves developed more intricate personalities. I grew away from drawing upon the actions of real little kids playing in sandboxes and riding tricycles." 1981

In the years before the Kite-Eating Tree, Charlie Brown's problem wasn't getting his kite to fly, it was finding enough running room—a recycled *Li'l Folks* gag. The house is like something from Wonderland. From the inside it's huge, on the outside it's tiny. "When I went to St. Paul for the first time, I was struck by how much of the neighborhood of his youth shows up in the strip." recalled Paige Braddock, "The overhang and stairs of the front stoop that he often drew look just like his childhood house."

Peanuts would become famous for denying its grown-ups a voice, but this panel from a 1952 Sunday strip shows a rare example of Schulz using adult dialogue, as Lucy negotiates with her mother regarding her baby brother Linus.

THE NURSERY WALL

Schulz painted this mural in 1951, for his daughter, Meredith, at the family's Colorado Spring home. Although Schulz himself thought the painting was "pretty lousy," the wall reveals a compelling example of early versions of some of the *Peanuts* characters. Charlie Brown and Snoopy are instantly recognizable, and Patty appears at the far left holding a balloon (see detail, right).

After the Schulz family moved in 1952, subsequent owners painted over this scene on at least four different occasions. In 1979 Polly and Stanley Travnicek purchased the house, with prior knowledge of the possible treasure lying beneath many layers of old latex. Once Mrs. Travnicek learned from Schulz that he created the mural with oil paints, she bought cans of sanding liquid and mountains of cotton balls, and set to work. She attacked the 96-square-foot wall one inch at a time, and nearly three months later the mural reappeared.

For years, the Travniceks preserved and shared the work with family, friends, and tour groups. Upon hearing of Schulz's health problems and impending retirement, they decided to donate the mural to the Charles M. Schulz Museum in Santa Rosa, California.

The entire wall was removed from the Travniceks' home in September 2001 and transported to Santa Rosa in a temperature-controlled truck. Upon its safe arrival, conservators prepared it for permanent exhibition by carefully cleaning it and filling in nearly fifty years' worth of nicks and scratches.

This detail of the nursery wall features an early version of Patty, as a blond. She usually appeared as a redhead, as on the cover of the first *Peanuts* comic book (right) issued by United Features Syndicate in 1952.

An early version of Snoopy, from a detail of the nursery wall, 1951. Opposite, right: Charlie Brown hops over a candlestick, from the same source.

Some of the earliest strips to appear in color, from the first *Peanuts* comic book, 1952. Note the dollop of orange that makes up Charlie Brown's hair.

PEANUTS

NICE TRY!

Another rare early strip, in color, from the first *Peanuts* comic book, 1952. Schulz almost certainly did not provide the color breakdowns, as the widely divergent schemes of the first two panels and the second two would seem to indicate. Also note that Charlie Brown doesn't have his zigzag shirt motif yet.

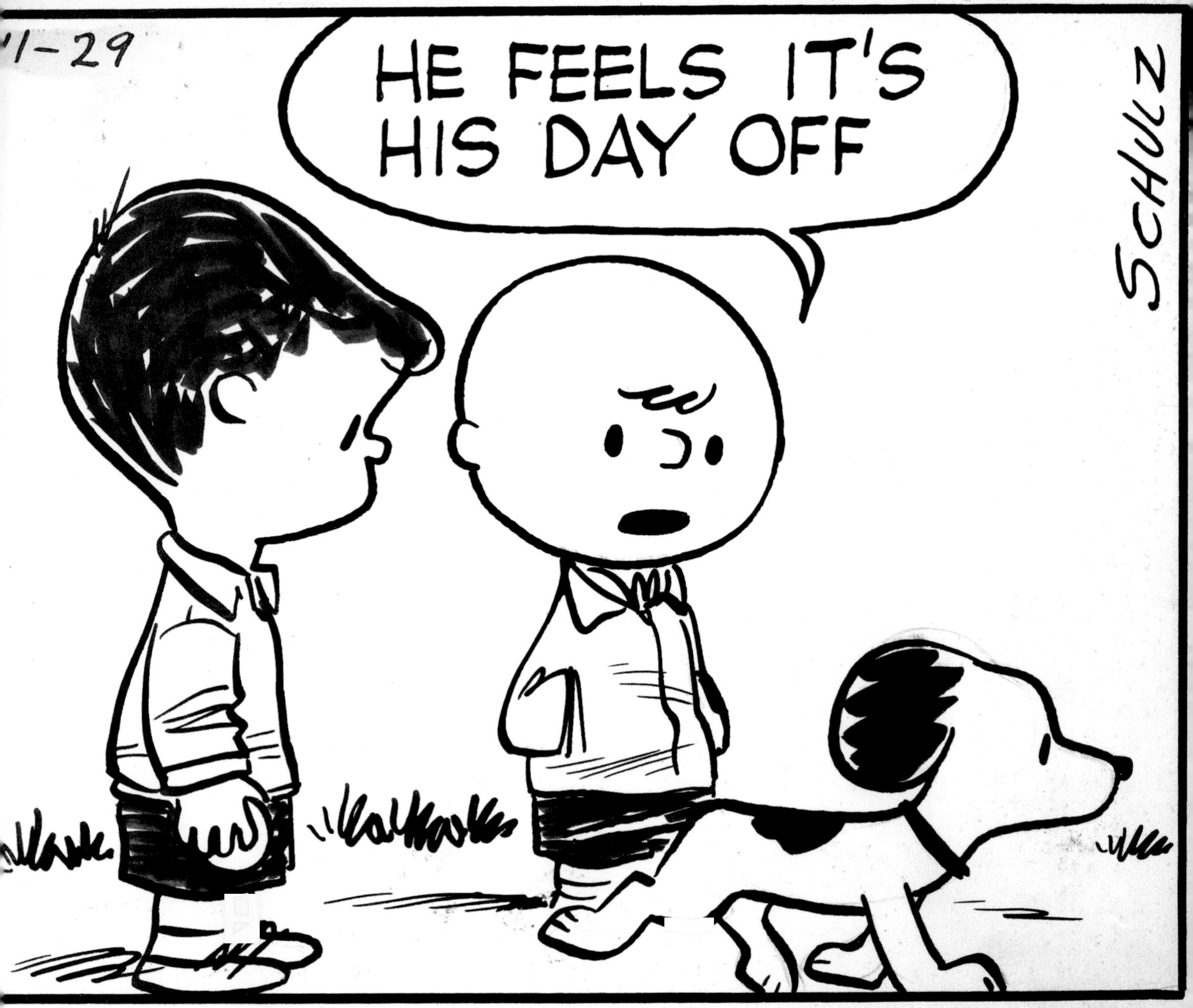
1-29
HE FEELS IT'S HIS DAY OFF
SCHULZ

PEANUTS

By **CHARLES M. SCHULZ**

RINEHART & CO., INCORPORATED

PRICE $1.00

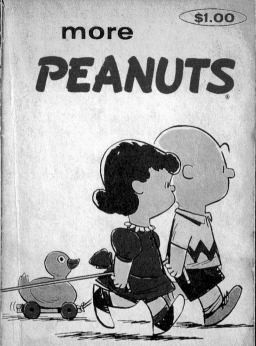

more PEANUTS

$1.00

by Charles M. Schulz

RINEHART & CO., INC.

Good Ol' CHARLIE BROWN

A NEW *PEANUTS*

$1.00

by *Charles M. Schulz*

RINEHART & COMPANY, INC.

The first collections of strips in book form were published by Rinehart & Co., Inc. Top, left to right: 1952, 1955, 1958. Right: *Peanuts* napkins, one of the first licensed products, produced by Monogram of California in 1958.

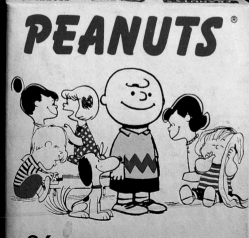

PEANUTS

36 NAPKINS *all different*

Opposite: Charlie Brown gets a jolt (from Snoopy, who's taking a bite out of the seat of his pants while playing a game of tag) in this detail from the very first Sunday strip, 1952. Above: Patty and Violet would have felt right at home with Pigpen in this original art for a Sunday strip, 1953.

Opposite: Baby Linus looks suspicious as Lucy extols the virtues of security blankets in this panel from an early Sunday strip, 1953. Left: The first Linus doll, from Hungerford Plastics, 1958. It's extremely difficult to find this or any of the Hungerford dolls in their original packaging, as shown here. Below: Another in the set of *Peanuts* napkins, Monogram of California, 1958.

The first Charlie Brown and Lucy dolls, by Hungerford Plastics, 1958, in their extremely rare original packages.

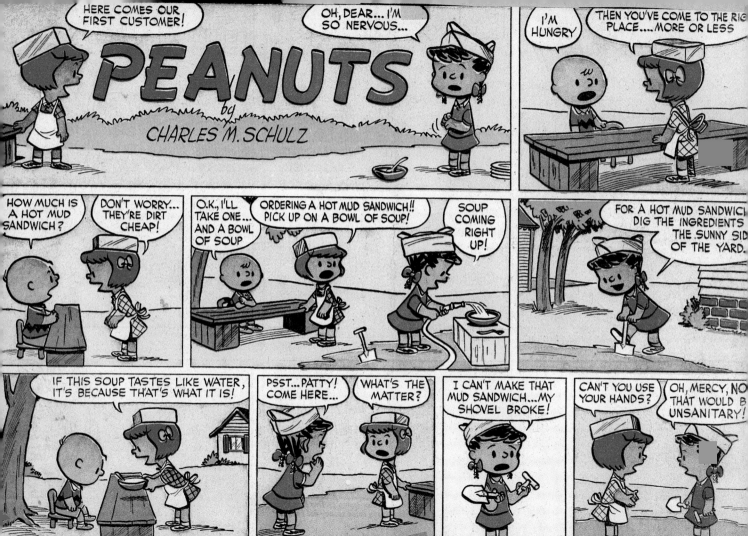

"PEANUTS"

MAD DOG! MAD DOG!!

WHAT A NICE GARDEN THIS MAN HAS!!

NOW WHO DREW THAT?

CHARLIE BROWN

A MAD DOG! SHOULDN'T WE CALL THE POLICE?

ISN'T IT WONDERFUL, CHARLIE BROWN?

WHAT AN INSULT! THAT'S NOT ME AT ALL!!

CHARLIE BROWN

NO, HE'S NOT THAT KIND OF A MAD DOG...

I THINK IT'S A WASTE OF GOOD LAND...

I'LL HAVE TO FIX THIS RIGHT AWAY

CHARLIE BROWN

HE'S JUST MAD AT CHARLIE BROWN!

HE SHOULD HAVE BUILT A BALL FIELD!

CHARLIE BROWN

With Lucy still a baby in 1953, someone had to boss the boys around, so Patty and Violet got the job. The ill-treatment of males by females was fair game in *Peanuts*, but *never* the other way around. Schulz said in 1967, "The supposedly weak people in the world are funny when they dominate the supposedly strong people. There is nothing funny about a little boy being mean to a little girl. That is simply not funny! But there is something funny about a little girl being mean to a little boy."

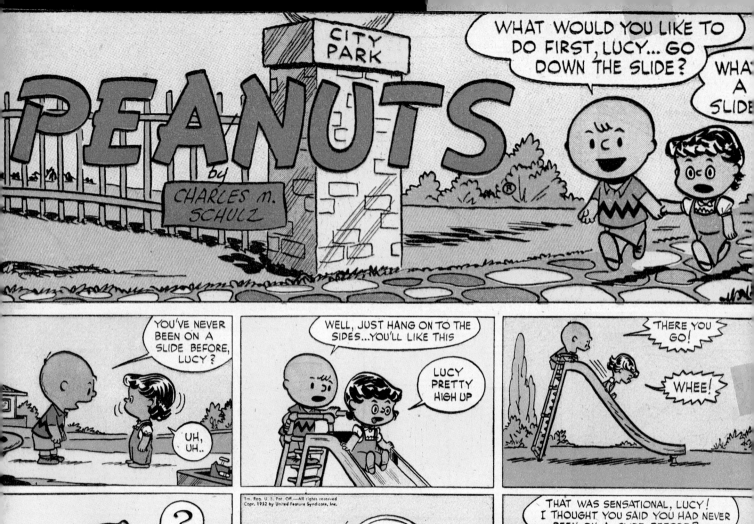

Linus, Lucy's baby brother, was introduced in September 1952, top. Charlie Brown still played a paternal role regarding Lucy, middle, and through Schroeder the idea of cultural snobbism was introduced, bottom.

Panel 1: HELLO,... SCHROEDER? I CALLED TO INVITE YOU TO MY PARTY...

Panel 2: I WAS WONDERING IF YOU'D BRING YOUR PIANO, AND PLAY FOR US...YOU WILL? GOOD...

Panel 3: I'VE ALSO INVITED A FELLOW WHO PLAYS THE ACCORDION, AND I'M SURE YOU AND HE...

Panel 4: HELLO? HELLO?

SCHULZ

14   233

Panel 1: BOY, I'M GLAD THAT'S OVER!

Panel 2: I DIDN'T THINK WE'D EVER GET 'EM OUT...

Panel 3: SIXTY-THREE RUNS IN THE VERY FIRST INNING!

Panel 4: THERE GOES OUR SHUTOUT!

SCHULZ

147   8-15

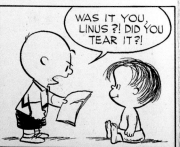

10/29

Panel 1: WHO TORE MY NEW COMIC MAGAZINE?!

Panel 2: WAS IT YOU, LINUS?! DID YOU TEAR IT?!

Panel 3: NOW, DON'T GO BLAMING LINUS..

Panel 4: HE'S JUST AN INNOCENT BY-SITTER!

Opposite, bottom: The concept of Charlotte Braun in 1954—a sort of female counterpart to Charlie Brown—came and went very quickly, and has become just another snippet of *Peanuts* trivia. The rigors of producing 365 cartoons a year meant that some of the ideas were bound to be better than others, but also forced Schulz to generate new material constantly, decide what worked, and proceed accordingly. In this case that meant discarding Charlotte, but keeping her voice—and eventually giving it to Lucy.

Yr Wendy — Charles M. Schulz

EANUTS"

Tm. Reg. U. S. Pat. Off.—All rights reserved
Copr. 1953 by United Feature Syndicate, Inc.

7-16

?

KLUNK!!

!

12-8

SCHULZ

EANUTS"

CHARLOTTE BRAUN, HUH? THAT'S A NICE NAME

ANY RELATION TO CHARLIE BROWN?

OH, GOOD GRIEF, NO!

!

ABSOLUTELY NOT! NO, SIR! NOT AT ALL! NO, SIRREE! ABSOLUTELY NOT!

ALL RIGHT! YOU DON'T HAVE TO BE SO INSISTENT!

12-1

SCHULZ

216

11-29

I'M THROUGH BEING PUSHED AROUND! DO YOU HEAR ME?!

I'M SICK AND TIRED OF ALWAYS BEING THE BASSOON!

THE WORD IS "BUFFOON"!

BEAT AGAIN!

SCHULZ

Snoopy often "thought" words, but he never actually spoke them, with the possible exception of this Sunday strip from 1952. The "pumpkin-headed" kid must be Charlie Brown, but who's wearing the hat? Opposite: Picasso was one of Schulz's favorite artists, and this undated sketch of Charlie Brown (probably mid-1950s) appears to bear his influence.

WHAT A BLOCKHEAD THAT CHARLIE BROWN IS!

I WONDER WHO EVER TOLD HIM HE COULD PITCH?! HE GETS WORSE EVERY INNING!

YOU'RE DOING GREAT, OL' PAL!! KEEP UP THE GOOD WORK!

92

WHAT A BLOCKHEAD THAT CHARLIE BROWN IS!

SCHULZ

4 eol

9-

C'MON OUT AN' PLAY...

SAY, "PLEASE"

PLEASE!

I CAN'T...MY MOTHER SAYS I HAVE TO STAY IN...

161

WE NEED A FOURTH FOR BRIDGE, CHARLIE BROWN...

WE HADN'T INTENDED TO ASK YOU, BUT WE COULDN'T FIND ANYONE ELSE...

AFTER LOOKING ALL OVER, WE FINALLY DECIDED ON YOU AS A LAST RESORT!

THERE'S NOTHING LIKE THE FEELING THAT YOU'RE REALLY WANTED!

SCHULZ

174

22

293

Compare the last panel in the above middle strip (1953) to the opposite page (1955). In the mid-50s Charlie Brown's head started to become less of a perfect oval (slightly wider at the bottom) and smaller in proportion to the rest of his body; and his eyes and "hair" sat higher on his face. This trend would continue through the 60s and on, giving him an increasingly mature, less baby-like appearance.

Schroeder's interest in music actually began with Charlie Brown. "The very first year the strip began I was looking through this book on music, and it showed a portion of Beethoven's Ninth in it, so I drew a cartoon of Charlie Brown singing this. I thought it looked kind of neat, showing these complicated notes coming out of the mouth of this comic-strip character, and I thought about it some more, and then I thought 'Why not have one of the little kids play a toy piano? Why not have Schroeder, who had just come into the strip as a baby, play it? That's how it all started. If I had known that it would work as well, I would have planned it more carefully." Schulz always drew all of the sheet music in the strip by hand.

182

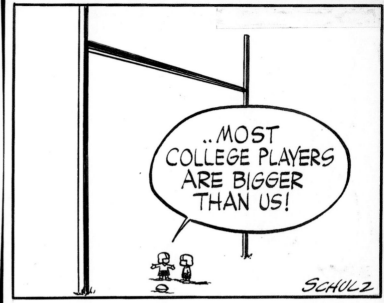

Schulz's original ending for this mid-1950s strip (below right) probably wasn't dramatic enough. The much more extreme solution (top right) was pasted on top of it, something he rarely did. At least (with Lucy nowhere in the vicinity) Charlie Brown got to kick the football.

This Schroeder doll is from the first line of licensed figures, produced by Hungerford Plastics Corp. in 1958 (see overleaf for the whole group). They came in two sizes, and Schroeder is considered the rarest because his piano was a separate piece that often got lost.

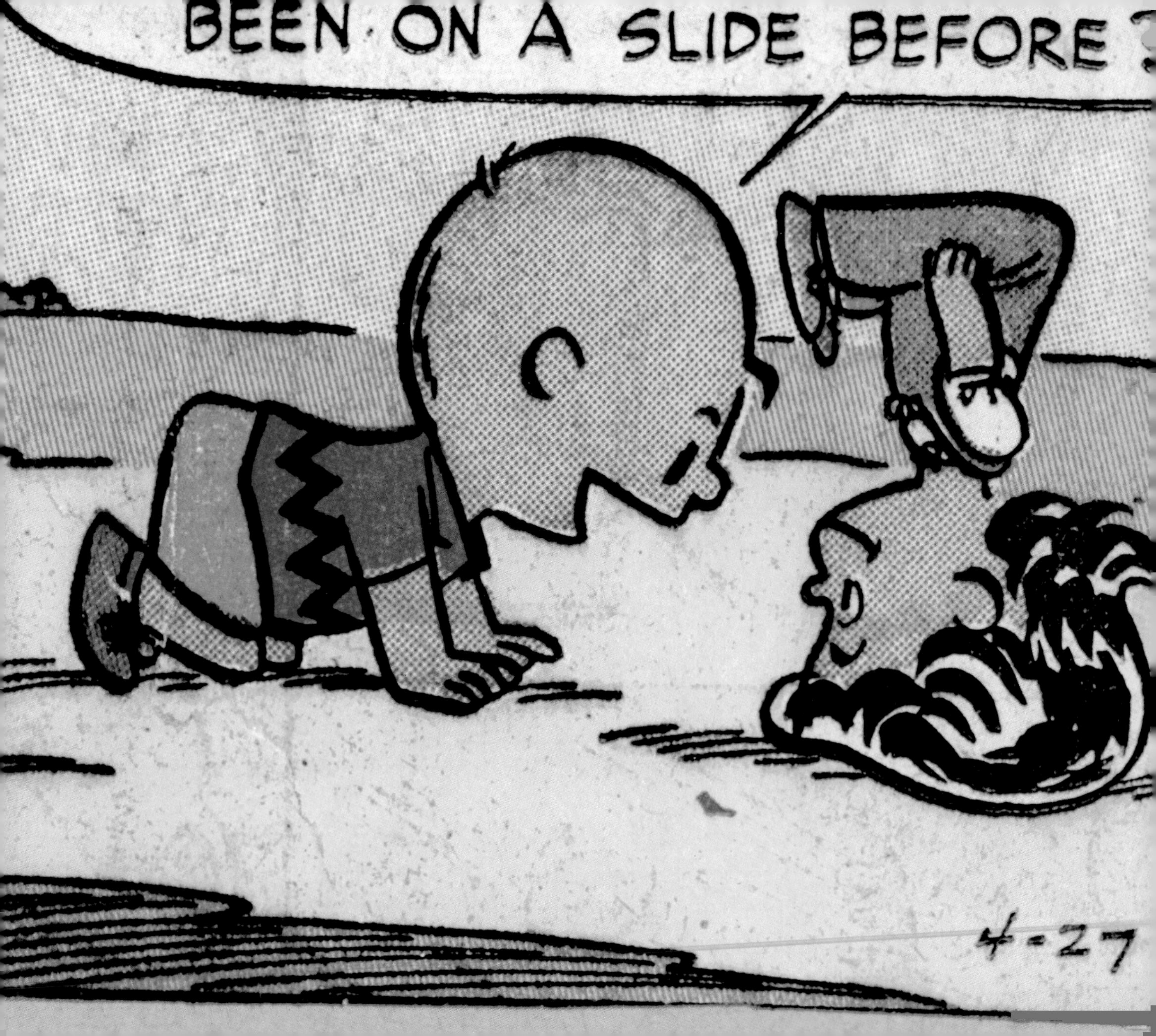
BEEN ON A SLIDE BEFORE?
4-27

IF THERE'S ANYTHING I CAN'T STAND, IT'S HAVING TO EAT BARE SOUP!!

BEAR SOUP?!

YEAH... THERE'S NOT A SINGLE CRACKER IN THE HOUSE...

SO I HAVE TO EAT BARE SOUP!

4

I WANT TO SHOW YOU MY NEW COMIC STRIP, SCHROEDER BECAUSE I THINK YOU'LL APPRECIATE IT..

THIS ONE MUSICIAN ASKS THE OTHER IF HE CAN PLAY THE "HALLELUJAH CHORUS," SEE? AND THIS GUY SAYS, 'OH, I GUESS I CAN **HANDEL** IT!'

GET IT? GET IT? PRETTY GOOD, HUH? HUH?!!

IT'S SORT OF SAD WHEN YOU THINK OF A KID LIKE THAT GOING THROUGH LIFE WITHOUT A SENSE OF HUMOR..

SCHULZ

7

"PEANUTS" THAT SNOWMAN IS JUST AS MUCH MINE AS IT IS YOURS!

IN FACT, CHARLIE BROWN... IF YOU DON'T LOOK OUT, I'M JUST LIABLE TO TAKE **MY** HALF, AND GO HOME!

OH, HO-HO-HO! YOU WOULDN'T DARE!

WOULDN'T I?

UH OH!

SCHULZ

Lucy's days as a charming baby were short-lived. Only a few years after her introduction in 1952, she grew to the same age as the other characters and became their peer. By the end of the 1950s she was the female star of the strip. Schulz found far more possibilities for her than for Violet or Patty, who all but vanished by the end of the 1960s.

Schulz said in 1966: "Little girls of that age are smarter than little boys and Lucy knows it better than most little girls. But she's not as smart as she thinks she is. Beneath the surface there's something tender. But perhaps if you scratched deeper you'd find she's even worse than she seems."

In what *has* to be the first use of the word "neurotic" in a daily comic strip (1954), Lucy calls a spade a spade. "You have to give her credit, though," Schulz said in a 1967 interview, "she has a way of cutting right down to the truth. This is one of her good points." And there aren't many. "Lucy is not a favorite [of mine] because I don't especially like her, that's all. But she *works*, and a central comic-strip character is not only one who fills his role very well, but who will provide ideas by the very nature of his personality. This is why Charlie Brown, Linus, Snoopy, and Lucy appear more than the others. Their personalities are so broad and flexible that they provide more ideas."

Schulz wrote in 1959, "I have always enjoyed working with Linus, who is Lucy's smaller brother, because I like to inject the naive things that he frequently comes up with. None of these characters could be doing or saying any of the things they do now when the strip first began, for it took many months and, in some cases, years, for them to develop these personalities."

And, in 1967, "Linus didn't come along for several years. He came because one day I was doodling on a piece of paper and I drew this little character with some wild hair straggling down from the top of his head and I showed it to a friend of mine who also was working at Art Instruction and whose name was Linus Maurer. For no reason at all I had written his name under it. He looked at it and we both kind of chuckled. Then I thought, why not put this character in the strip and make him Lucy's brother?"

Though it was first and foremost a newspaper strip, the popularity of *Peanuts* made its appearance in comic books inevitable. In 1952, *Peanuts* strips began appearing in such titles as *Tip Top Comics* and *United Comics*, comic books published by United Feature featuring its properties. The only time Schulz ever relinquished creating comics that featured his characters was for Dell and Gold Key comic books in the late 1950s and early 1960s. "Because it gave me a chance to have a couple of

friends do something." he said, in 1997. Namely Jim Sasseville and Dale Hale, two friends from Art Instruction that Schulz had brought with him to California. Schulz was adamant that he never used assistants on the strip, and considered the comic

book stories to be completely separate from it. The real re-print life of *Peanuts* was not to be comics, but paperback books. First published in 1952 by Rinehart and Co., to date there are over an astonishing 200 million *Peanuts* strip collections in print

PEANUTS

by CHARLES M. SCHULZ

IT'S GONE!

OF ALL THE NERVE!

GO AHEAD... JUMP!

I'M SCARED!

THERE'S NOTHING TO BE SCARED OF, LUCY... YOU'VE GOT THAT UMBRELLA TO HELP YOU

THAT'S TRUE...

TIP TOP COMICS

PEANUTS

by CHARLES M. SCH

LUCY'S TAKEN MY BASEBALL GLOVE AGAIN!

JUST BECAUSE I LEAVE IT ON THE FRONT SIDEWALK EVERY NIGHT, SHE THINKS IT'S PUBLIC PROPERTY!

I'M GOING TO SETTLE THIS ONCE AND FOR ALL...

INSTEAD OF JUMPING I THINK I'LL CLOSE MY EYES, AND JUST STEP OFF

?

I DID IT! I'M FLOATING IN THE AIR! I'M FLOATING IN THE AIR!!

HEY YOU!!..

THUMP!

? !

KLOP!

I'M GOING TO DO THAT AGAIN...

JUST THINK...I WAS FLOATING IN THE AIR!

YOU'D PROBABLY BE BETTER OFF IF YOU'D QUIT RIGHT NOW

ARE YOU CRAZY A SUCCESS! WITH UMBRELLA I CAN IN THE AIR!!

PLUNK!

CLUMP!

OH, DO YOU WANT YOUR GLOVE BACK, CHARLIE BROWN?

NO, YOU MIGHT AS WELL KEEP IT, LUCY.... I'LL PROBABLY NEVER HAVE ANY USE FOR IT AGAIN!

THIS IS GETTING OUT OF HAND...I THINK I'LL LEAVE, TOO...

HERE I GO AGAIN!

THUMP

I'M GLAD I DIDN'T SEE THAT...

PEANUTS
by CHARLES M. SCHULZ

34

4col

WE'LL PRETEND THE INDIANS ARE COMING, SEE?

WE'LL PRETEND THAT THEY CAPTURE YOU, AND THAT THEY TIE YOU TO A STAKE...

AND THEN WE'LL PRETEND THAT..

HOLD IT! I DON'T THINK I'LL PLAY..

I CAN GET A BETTER ROLE IN THE PIRATES GAME GOING ON ACROSS THE STREET..

160

27

1-28

The fact that Snoopy seems to be "speaking" here, rather than "thinking" in a thought balloon, is most likely just an oversight.

When asked in an interview in 1977 if he ever created a character who became more popular than he would have liked, Schulz surprisingly answered Pig-Pen. "Everybody kind of likes Pig-Pen. I don't like to draw him. He's only useful if you have him involved in dust and being dirty. I don't have many ideas on that; I ran out of them. People are always asking 'Why don't you draw Pig-Pen?'"

Introduced in July of 1954, Pig-Pen was a kind of vaudevillian figure who existed solely to become filthy. Somehow, a lot of people related to that—like the sensation of a pebble caught in your shoe feeling like a boulder.

YOU'RE SLOWING DOWN, "PIG-PEN."

WAIT A MINUTE...I THINK THERE'S SOME SAND IN MY SHOES...

Tm. Reg. U. S. Pat. Off.—All rights reserved
Copr. 1958 by United Feature Syndicate, Inc.

THERE...THAT'S BETTER!

I JUST CAN'T RUN IF I HAVE SOMETHING IN MY SHOE...

8-10

good grief!

SCHULZ

This 1958 Hungerford Pig-Pen doll arrived on store shelves, curiously enough, clean as a whistle—probably a marketing decision.

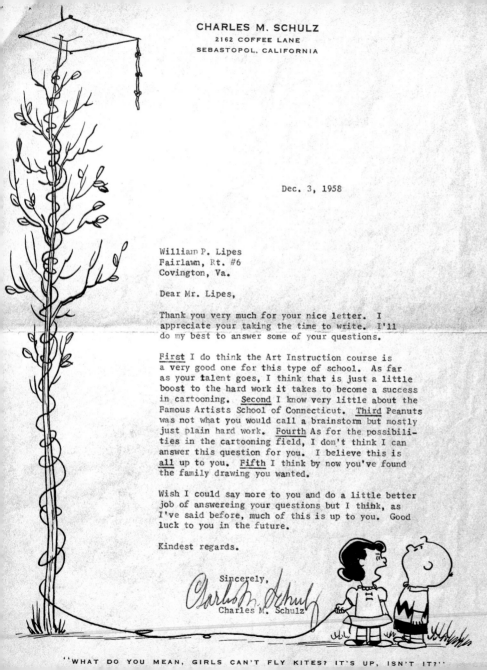

CHARLES M. SCHULZ
2162 COFFEE LANE
SEBASTOPOL, CALIFORNIA

Dec. 3, 1958

William P. Lipes
Fairlawn, Rt. #6
Covington, Va.

Dear Mr. Lipes,

Thank you very much for your nice letter. I appreciate your taking the time to write. I'll do my best to answer some of your questions.

First I do think the Art Instruction course is a very good one for this type of school. As far as your talent goes, I think that is just a little boost to the hard work it takes to become a success in cartooning. Second I know very little about the Famous Artists School of Connecticut. Third Peanuts was not what you would call a brainstorm but mostly just plain hard work. Fourth As for the possibilities in the cartooning field, I don't think I can answer this question for you. I believe this is all up to you. Fifth I think by now you've found the family drawing you wanted.

Wish I could say more to you and do a little better job of answereing your questions but I think, as I've said before, much of this is up to you. Good luck to you in the future.

Kindest regards.

Sincerely,

Charles M. Schulz
Charles M. Schulz

"WHAT DO YOU MEAN, GIRLS CAN'T FLY KITES? IT'S UP, ISN'T IT?"

Left: Schulz encourages a fan, on stationery that features the Kite Eating Tree, one of Charlie Brown's greatest nemeses.

Opposite: Schulz did not draw this comic book story, from *Tip Top Comics*, 1958. Note how oddly wrong it feels to have what is usually contained in four or six panels go on for pages. Also, it shows just how deceptively simple Schulz's style is and yet impossible to copy.

Below: It simply isn't meant to be. Charlie Brown finally gets his kite to fly and the sheer impossibility of it causes spontaneous combustion. 1958.

SIGNALS! ONE! SIX! THREE! TWO! FIVE! HIKE!

TIME OUT!

SAY, CHARLIE BROWN... ABOUT THE WAY YOU CALL THOSE SIGNALS..

I THINK YOU SHOULD TRY MIXING UP THE NUMBERS INSTEAD OF SAYING THEM IN THEIR RIGHT ORDER!

177

288

282

4 col

"EANUTS" THIS OLD PIECE OF PAPER CAN BE FIRST BASE

NOW, YOU STAND RIGHT ON TOP OF IT, LUCY... THAT'S THE WAY..

YOU MEAN YOU WANT ME TO PLAY FIRST BASE?

NO, YOU JUST STAND THERE, AND KEEP THE PAPER FROM BLOWING AWAY!

"EANUTS" LUCY..

YES, MOTHER?

YOU STOP THAT FUSSING RIGHT NOW, AND EAT YOUR SUPPER!

WELL! WHAT AN INSULT!

I WASN'T FUSSING... I WAS SINGING!

This Sunday strip from 1954 is reprinted here for the first time. Schulz apparently considered it a failed experiment and never had it collected in a book. It's one of a four-part series of Sunday strips featuring Charlie Brown and Lucy at a golf tournament with—gasp!—adults. Schulz took Charlie Brown's advice and chose to forget about them.

Opposite, top: Undated Art Instruction Inc. Christmas card from the mid-1950s, featuring the work of its star pupil and instructor.

Opposite, bottom: The use of repetition in this holiday strip from 1958 heightens the sense of Linus's anxiety. In the end, threats will make you remember anything.

PEANUTS

8-11

HELLO, SNOOPY? CAN YOU COME OVER RIGHT AWAY?

DID I JUST HEAR YOU CALL UP A DOG? AND ON A TOY TELEPHONE?

THAT'S THE MOST RIDICULOUS THING I'VE EVER HEARD!

GLAD TO SEE YOU, SNOOPY... I KNEW YOU'D COME IF I ASKED YOU....

SCHULZ

144

283

WE'RE GOING TO HAVE A PARTY AND WE'RE **NOT** GOING TO INVITE YOU!!

THAT'S A GOOD IDEA... I THINK YOU'RE DOING THE RIGHT THING...

IF I HAVE THE TYPE OF PERSONALITY THAT ANNOYS YOU, IT WOULD BE SILLY TO INVITE ME..

SCHULZ

29

1-29

EANUTS"
WHAT ARE YOU READING, CHARLIE BROWN?
NONE OF YOUR BUSINESS

WHAT IS IT ABOUT?
NONE OF YOUR BUSINESS

MAY I SEE IT?

Tm. Reg. U. S. Pat. Off.—All rights reserved
Copr. 1954 by United Feature Syndicate, Inc.
SCHULZ
4-15
NONE OF YOUR BUSINESS

"PEANUTS"

OWOOOOOO

"PEANUTS" WELL! THAT'S THE MOST FEEBLE MOON HOWLING I'VE EVER HEARD!

WHAT DO YOU EXPECT? OWOOOOOO

IT'S ONLY A **HALF**-MOON!

5-17

"PEANUTS"

?

5-18

RATS!

"PEANUTS" HI,'PIG-PEN' HI, CHARLIE BROWN...GOT SOME CANDY, EH? GONNA GIMME SOME?

LET'S SEE...I'LL FEEL AROUND A BIT UNTIL I FIND A PIECE I LIKE.. OOPS! I SQUASHED ONE..

SOME OF THESE ARE KIND OF STICKY, AREN'T THEY? THAT DOESN'T MATTER, THOUGH....MY HANDS WERE STICKY TO START WITH..

WELL, THAT WAS NICE OF HIM...HE WALKED AWAY AND LEFT ME THE WHOLE BAG!

SCHU 7-

"PEANUTS" "A MUSIC PUBLISHER CAME TO BEETHOVEN ONE DAY, AND OFFERED HIM FIFTY DOLLARS FOR A NEW PIECE.."

" 'MY PRICE IS ONE HUNDRED DOLLARS,' SAID BEETHOVEN.."

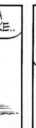

" 'FIFTY DOLLARS,' SAID THE PUBLISHER,'AND NOT ONE CENT MORE!' "

DON'T LET HIM BLUF YOU, BEETHOVEN!

HI, 'PIG-PEN'

HI, CHARLIE BROWN...GOT SOME CANDY, EH? GONNA GIMME SOME?

LET'S SEE...I'LL FEEL AROUND A BIT UNTIL I FIND A PIECE I LIKE.. OOPS! I SQUASHED ONE..

SOME OF THESE ARE KIND OF STICKY, AREN'T THEY? THAT DOESN'T MATTER, THOUGH...MY HANDS WERE STICKY TO START WITH..

WELL, THAT WAS NICE OF HIM... HE WALKED AWAY AND LEFT ME THE WHOLE BAG!

SCHULZ 7-22

In 1959 the Lego Company of Germany produced the second series of *Peanuts* figures, with nodding heads attached to their bodies by springs. They made Charlie Brown, Snoopy, Lucy, Linus, Schroeder and Pig-Pen (left)—this time complete with dirt.

"I have affixed to me the dust of countless ages. Who am I to disturb history?"
—Pig-Pen, 1955

Opposite: Schulz deviates from his strict four-panel configuration in 1954 (though with the same proportions so it can be rearranged like the others), as Lucy tries to rise above it all . Also, compare the original art of Charlie Brown being grossed out with that of the printed strip from the newspaper—Pig-Pen must have been handling the printing press, too.

PIG PEN
OF THE PEANUTS COMIC STRIP

229

PEANUTS
AND SNOOPY
SUPER SLATE

8814
39¢

FROM THE FAMOUS
COMIC STRIP
CREATED BY
CHARLES M. SCHULZ

DRAW
THEN
LIFT FILM

CRAYON FU[N]
ON BACK

Authorized
Edition

This "super slate" is one of the first licensed toys, from the early 1960s.
Schulz probably did not do the art for Snoopy and Charlie Brown, whose
zigzag motif extends to his socks.

7½ wide + 9½ wide   50 .H1683   358/276

At first Lucy wasn't any worse than her friends Violet and Patty, all of whom took delight in tormenting Charlie Brown when the mood struck. But at some point Lucy pulled ahead of the pack and then *no one* was safe (above right, 1958).

Schulz claimed that Lucy was the outlet for the darker nature of his personality. One of the scariest things about her was the ease with which she could shift from friendly to venomous. Just like real people.

PEANUTS
by CHARLES M. SCHULZ

...RE A CHEAT
A LIAR AND
FOOL!

BOY, JUST LISTEN TO THOSE INSULTS! VIOLET HAS LUCY SPEECHLESS...SHE REALLY KNOWS HOW TO DIG HER!

YOU HAVE A FACE LIKE A **GOAT**! NO, I TAKE THAT BACK...YOU LOOK MORE LIKE A **BABOON**!

...T LISTEN TO HER... ...GLAD IT'S NOT **ME** ...S YELLING AT... I'D ...ER BE ABLE TO ...AKE IT!

SHE'S GOOD ALL RIGHT... THERE'S NO DENYING THAT..

...BUT JUST WAIT UNTIL THEY GET UP CLOSE...

...RE A NO-GOOD, TALE-TATTLING LITTLE ...AKING SNIP-SNAP PONY-TAILED APE!!!

NOBODY CAN BEAT LUCY AT **INFIGHTING**!

WORLD'S NUMBER 1 FUSSBUDGET

CHAMP

...RITISH OPEN FUSSBUDGET CHAMPIONSHIP

WESTERN OPEN

STATE CHAMP 1

NATIONAL CHAMPION

CHAMP

LUCY
OF THE PEANUTS COMIC STRIP

The Lucy "nodder" figure (1959) is unusual because she actually looks crabby. Licensees tended to produce "happy" versions of the characters.

The Ford Motor Company was the first major advertising licensee for the *Peanuts* characters in 1960, but it was more than that—it spawned the first animated versions of the characters, which led to a lifelong partnership between Schulz and animator Bill Melendez.

Melendez was at Playhouse Pictures, a cartoon studio that mostly made commercials and listed Ford as its biggest client. A Melendez-animated Charlie Brown made his TV debut in 1959, on ads for the Ford Falcon, and the rest of the gang soon followed—all in black and white.

Not long after, documentary producer Lee Mendelson was putting together a short film called *A Boy Named Charlie Brown* and wanted an animated sequence. He brought on Melendez, and with Schulz, they formed a team that put together *A Charlie Brown Christmas* in 1965. More than thirty animated specials followed, in as many years.

WITH ALL THESE OPTIONS, YOU CAN BUILD YOUR FALCON AS DELUXE AS YOU LIKE!

FALCON

FORD
'61 Falcon
WORLD'S MOST
SUCCESSFUL NEW CAR
NEW MEASURE OF COMPACT CAR VALUE
SCHULZ
Peanuts Characters © 1950, 1959 United Feature Syndicate, Inc.

2-29

The arrival of Charlie Brown's little sister Sally in June 1959 (and her first appearance that August) changed the dynamic of his life as a loner—at least in his own home. At first he was almost fatherly with her, as he was with Lucy. And like Lucy, Sally didn't stay a baby for long. Soon she'd learn to walk, talk, and develop a crush on Linus, much to his chagrin. She also made demands on her big brother, like this example from the early 1990s:

Sally: "School starts next week. I need you to test me on my multiplication tables."
Charlie Brown: "Okay, how much is five times eight?"
Sally: "Who cares?"
Charlie Brown: "I think you're ready."

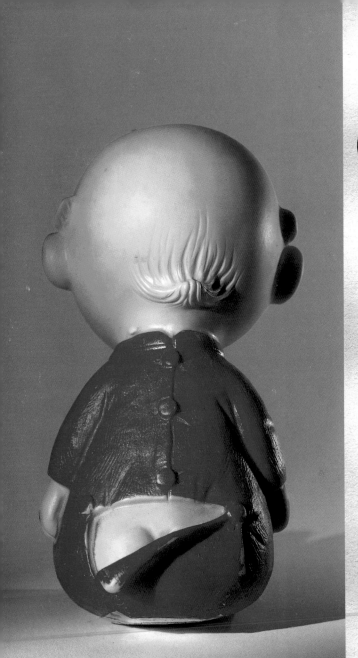

by Charles M. Schulz

Peanuts **thrives** on unrequited love: Charlie Brown's for the Little Red-haired Girl, Sally's for Linus, Linus's for his teacher Miss Othmar, and of course, Lucy's for Schroeder. For over thirty years she lay back, leaned on his piano, and threw herself at him.

SCHROEDER
OF THE PEANUTS COMIC STRIP

You didn't send me a valentine this year...

I'm well aware of that

May I ask you why you didn't send me a valentine this year?

I didn't want to give you the wrong impression..

What do you mean?

Sending a valentine would have implied that I can stand the sight of you!

I think there must be a music school someplace where musicians go to learn harmony, counterpoint and sarcasm!

As with so much else in the strip, her lack of success was part of any reader's own life. And it gave Lucy a much-needed soft spot that made her sympathetic. At least in *this* situation.

...hat do you mean, he wasn't so great?

Just what I said!

He was the greatest composer who ever lived!

Phooey!

He never got to be club champion, did he? Huh? Did he?!

This is the only known drawing by Schulz of the Little Red-Haired Girl, from 1950. In 1947 Donna Johnson began working in the accounting department of Art Instruction Inc. Schulz became smitten, and a long romance ensued. When he proposed, however, she refused him and married fireman Allan Wold instead. Schulz was devastated, but he remained friends with her for the rest of his life, and he drew on his unfulfilled love to produce one of the most poignant storylines in *Peanuts*.

The device of never actually seeing the Little Red-Haired Girl brilliantly underscored Charlie Brown's hopeless longing for her. And besides, as Schulz admitted in 1997, "I could never draw her to satisfy the readers' impression of what she's probably like."

This is a cartoon Sparky drew left on my desk at Art Instruction. The numbers are for my shorthand class for that day and the year was 1950.

*Donna Wold
the little red-haired girl*

This note to a Peanuts collector explains the numbers scrawled on the drawing on the opposite page.

Above, right: Schulz and Donna Wold in the 1980s.

THAT LITTLE RED-HAIRED GIRL HAS MOVED AWAY, AND I'LL NEVER SEE HER AGAIN...

"They say that opposites attract . . . She's really something and I'm really nothing . . . How opposite can you get?"
—CHARLIE BROWN, 1963

HOW CAN YOU THINK ABOUT EATING AT A TIME LIKE THIS?! DON'T YOU HAVE **ANY** SENTIMENTALITY?

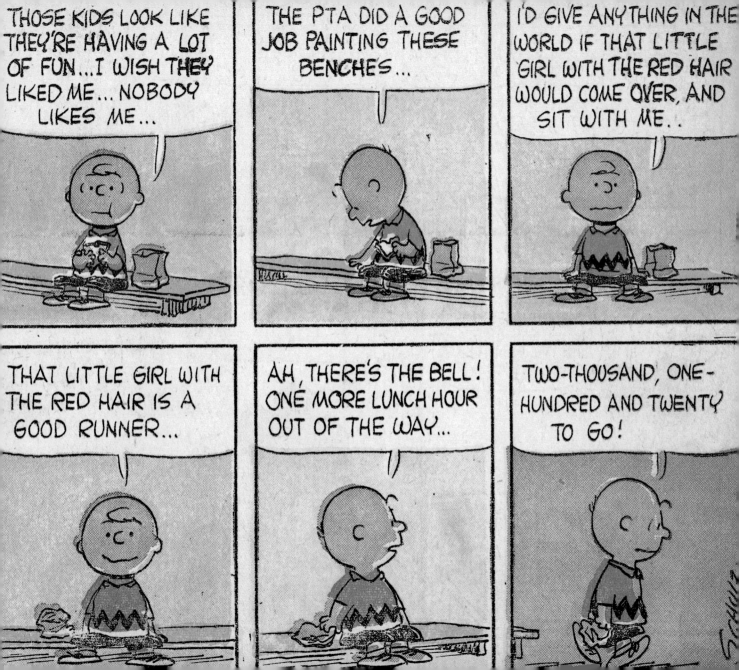

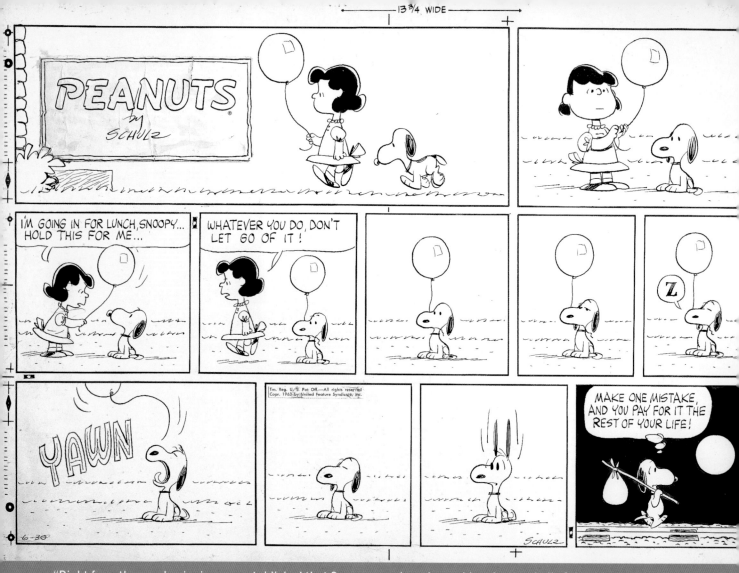

"Right from the very beginning, we established that Snoopy as a dog who could understand all of the things which the children were saying to him. He also has a very highly developed sense of intelligence and frequently resents the things the children say about him. He definitely has a mind of his own, and expresses it in thoughts and action." —C. M. S., 1959

PEANUTS

AUTHORIZED EDITION

®

88
29

SUPER SLATE FUN

1ST
STAGE

FROM ... AMOUS COMIC STRIP
BY CHARLES M. SCHULZ

DRAW
THE
LIF
FIL

**CRAYO
FUN
ON
BACK**

"A cartoonist is someone who has to draw the same thing
every day without repeating himself."

—C. M. SCHULZ, 1984

PEANUTS

NO, THAT'S TOO LOOSE...I FEEL FLIMSY...

HOW'S THAT?

TOO TIGHT! TOO TIGHT! AAUGH!

ALL RIGHT, HOW'S THAT?

WHEW! THAT'S FINE! YES, THAT'S FINE! WHEW!

I CAN'T EVEN BREATHE IF MY SHOELACES AREN'T TIED JUST RIGHT!

5-13

To Judy with every best wish — Charles M. Schulz

PEANUTS

FRIEDA! COME, AND GET YOUR CAT!!

THIS IS TERRIBLE...I CAN'T CARRY THIS CAT AROUND FOR THE REST OF MY LIFE...

THAT DIRTY CHARLIE BROWN! THIS WAS **HIS** WORK! HE WAS THE ONE WHO TRICKED ME!

AND THE LEAST **YOU** COULD DO IS LOOK A LITTLE **GUILTY**!!

6-8

PEANUTS

YES, WE'LL RALLY ROUND THE FLAG, BOYS...

WE ARE A BAND OF BROTHERS AND NATIVE TO THE SOIL...

JUST BEFORE THE BATTLE, MOTHER

I'LL BE GLAD WHEN THE CENTENNIAL IS OVER!

7-8

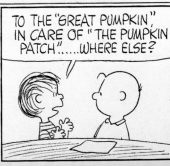

PEANUTS

ALL RIGHT, SO WE WRITE A LETTER TO THE GREAT PUMPKIN TELLING HIM WHAT WE WANT HIM TO BRING US...

WHERE DO WE SEND IT?

TO THE "GREAT PUMPKIN," IN CARE OF "THE PUMPKIN PATCH"......WHERE ELSE?

WHERE ELSE, INDEED?

10-26

Opposite, right: Linus and his security blanket, on a wall plaque from the mid 1960s. Schulz said in 1977 "[The security blanket] came, of course, from our first three children. And again it wasn't plotted very carefully at first because I think even Charlie Brown had a blanket in one or two sequences. But it worked out well, and that is probably the single best thing that I ever thought of. 'Security blanket' is now in the dictionary."

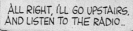

"Sucking your thumb without a blanket is like eating a cone without ice cream!"

— LINUS, 1964

Of the torment Lucy puts Linus through, Schulz said in 1997, "You know, the kids in the strip—it's kind of a parody of the cruelty that exists among children. Because they are struggling to survive."

Opposite: An undated sketch, probably from the mid-1950s, of an unusually retaliatory Linus

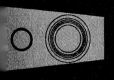

THE BROWNIE BOOK of Picture-taking

The Brownie Book of Picture-taking

The very first *Peanuts* licensee was Kodak, for its Brownie camera, in 1955. This brochure featured the entire *Peanuts* cast.

a Kodak publication

Nothing's easy the first time you try.

Sometimes not even the second or the third. Making really good snapshots is no different. There just isn't a magic formula.

If you punch the camera button as if you're angry at it, or take flash shots with the same batteries that were in the flash holder a year ago, you're likely to end up with the snapshot equivalent of O-D-G, which doesn't spell much of anything, least of all a good picture.

But there's a big advantage on your side. Brownie Cameras know how to make wonderful snapshots. It's just a matter of getting acquainted with the few easy tricks you need for helping them out.

Just read through this booklet, start snapping away, and pretty soon all the good habits will begin coming out in exactly the right order to spell D-O-G (or anything else you'd like to spell) every time.

contents

illustrated by Charles M. Schulz, creator of the comic strip, PEANU

KODALITE FLASHOLDER (Lumaclad Reflector)

FILM	LAMP-TO-SUBJECT DISTANCE (IN FEET)	
	SM OR SF LAMP	NO. 5 OR NO. 25 LAMP
VERICHROME	FROM 5 TO 10	FROM 6 TO 18
KODACOLOR*	5	FROM 5 TO 9

KODALITE MIDGET FLASHOLDER

FILM	LAMP-TO-SUBJECT DISTANCE (IN FEET)	
	M2 LAMP	NO. 5 OR NO. 25 LAMP
VERICHROME	FROM 5 TO 10	FROM 5 TO 10
KODACOLOR*	FROM 3 TO 4†	FROM 3 TO 4†

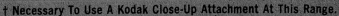

† Necessary To Use A Kodak Close-Up Attachment At This Range.
* Do Not Use Film Marked "Kodacolor Film, Daylight Type."

HOW I SOLD 1,000,000 FALCONS (IN MY SPARE TIME)

by CHARLIE BROWN

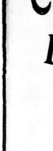

Life in a comic strip may look like fun but, good grief, some days it can just make you feel grim. Imagine having to stand around, the way I do sometimes, holding my kite string and trying to look significant.

Those are the days when you realize how important it is to have a hobby. A hobby can make you forget the workaday world. A hobby can make new friends for you. Even for me. I figure I made a million new friends with my hobby, selling Falcons.

Falcons are more fun than kites . . . they work! And there's certainly no fuss about selling them. Most people recognize a good thing when they see it—especially with me in the Falcon ads.

I do like to feel that the Falcon and I grew up together. Of course, things grow faster than children. I could have predicted that Falcon would be America's best selling compact car, right from the start. Nobody ever asked me, though.

MEET THE MAN BEHIND CHARLIE BROWN

From the drawing board pictured above frolics a lovable little group of cartoon character children who appear in over 400 newspapers . . . and in Falcon ads as well. They have won for Charlie Schulz such impressive titles as "Humorist of the Year" and "Cartoonist of the Year."

For some twelve years now, Cartoonist Schulz has been expressing his special brand of wry philosophy through his bright-eyed brood . . . and especially through his hero, Charlie Brown. Without perennial scapegoat Charlie, nagging Lucy, her brother, security-seeking Linus, and talented, unappreciated Snoopy the dog, more than 38 million readers would feel that something was missing from their lives.

It's a long way to have come for this unassuming young man who started out teaching art for $65 a week. His sense of unimportance developed early in life. Charles Schulz, boy wonder, was grade-skipped too often during his elementary school days. Finding himself outclassed in high school both scholastically and socially, he barely squeaked through—after flunking algebra, English, Latin, physics and dating. Even the cartoons he submitted for his yearbook were rejected. Schulz recalls his feelings during this period, "I just waited for three o'clock to arrive and got back to my own neighborhood where things were better."

Although things may not always seem better for Charlie Brown in his own neighborhood, it is significant that he and his friends never venture outside the limits of their little community. Artist Schulz told us that his philosophy of life extends into the realms of art and humor as well. For this reason, we see no Mr. and Mrs. Brown, no local schoolhouse, no cookie jar . . . simply the little children and their reactions to one another. From there the reader's imagination may turn to his own childhood, to his adulthood, or to his children . . . Schulz's characters lead universal lives.

Charles Schulz, himself, lives with his wife and five very real children on 28 acres of "Coffee Grounds" on Coffee Lane in Sebastopol, California. Schulz teaches Sunday School, devotes most of his spare time to golf, and has never been heard to utter anything more blasphemous than "rats" and "good grief," two of Charlie Brown's favorite expressions.

The nicest thing about Charles Schulz is that he turns out to be exactly the nice guy you'd like him to be. With characteristic Schulz generosity, he broke away from his busy work schedule to give us all the time we needed, answering all of our questions in between receiving business calls and callers, chatting with his children, and getting out his daily strip.

Interruptions are par for the course. And, over lunch, Schulz wondered aloud whether one day he would open his newspaper to find that he hadn't finished "Peanuts" in time, and that a blank space was appearing instead. With all the demands made on him however, the man behind Charlie Brown just can't seem to help being interested in everything around him . . . and letting Charlie Brown tell the world all about it!

HAVE YOU GOT IT, CHARLIE BROWN?
DON'T MISS IT!
GET UNDER IT, CHARLIE BROWN!
ISN'T THIS EXCITING?
WHAT IF HE DROPS IT?
IF HE DROPS IT, LET'S ALL KICK HIM!

CharLie BrownS
FALCON NEWS

P.O. BOX NO. 1056, DETROIT 31, MICH.

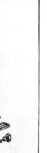

PRESS
CUB

SCHULZ

ARF
ARF

FULLY ALUMINIZED MUFFLER
LASTS LONGER!

A SCRaPbook
about YOUR FalcOn

PREPARED BY CHARLIE BROWN AND HIS FRIENDS

J. Walter Thompson Company News

CONFIDENTIAL BULLETIN—FOR STAFF MEMBERS ONLY

Vol. XV, No. 43   October 26, 1960

"Good grief it's 'Peanuts'"

STARS OF RENOWNED COMIC STRIP AND FORD FALCON ADVERTISING IN NYO THIS WEEK

New York...Lovers of Charlie Brown and Company are having a field day in New York Office this week with the current display of Charles Schulz's famous "Peanuts" characters. Exhibited are some samples from the artist's comic strip — past, present and future — some interesting information on the talented Mr. Schulz (above) plus some sample proofs and artwork from the very successful Ford Falcon campaign featuring Charlie Brown and his friends.

For the past year the "Peanuts" comic strip characters have spoken for Ford in all media. Mr. Schulz is as much interested in the advertising campaigns as he is in his comic strip. He works closely with Thompson art directors and writers to make sure that the "Peanuts" characters are faithfully reproduced, and are as amusing selling Ford Falcons as they are in their comic strip escapades. The Thompson team which helps write the dialogue and does the rough layouts are concerned, too, with the faithful reproduction of the characters as well as the quality of the advertising and how well the selling message gets across.

For the TV commercials it's interesting to note that the voices of the "Peanuts" characters are real children, aged six and eight. In order to find just the right voices for each character, Thompson screened dozens of children's voices in New York and Hollywood, finally choosing three from the East Coast and two from the West Coast to make up the cast. The sixth character, the dog Snoopy, never speaks on TV. Mr. Schulz was very actively engaged in this search for voices, making the final selections himself.

Mr. Schulz will be visiting NYO today before going to Detroit to tour the Ford plant and address the Ad Craft club. Renowned in his field, he was named "Cartoonist of the Year" in 1956 by the National Cartoonist Society and received the "Humorist of the Year" award in 1958 from the Yale Record. His comic strip is read by 18 million people daily and an amusing sign of its immense popularity is seen in an incident that happened recently. The Detroit Free Press inadvertently omitted the strip from the first two editions one day and as the editor explained in a front-page story "Our switchboard lit up like a Christmas tree... We stopped the presses — just like in the movies — and got "Peanuts" back in the paper."

Falcon '61

By Charles M. Schulz

By Charles M. Schulz

New Measure of Compact Car Value

NOT OK FOR PRODUCTION

NY AUGUST 17, 1960

NUTS LOVE"
FORD CAR COMMERCIAL
CHEDULED
INUTES - COLOR FILM - #61-70

EO

MATION

OPEN ON CHARLIE BROWN, PIG PEN
LINUS BESIDE A HUGE RED HEART
PLAYED IN A FORD SHOWROOM. IT
DS "EVERYONE LOVES THE FALCON"
OUR DOOR DELUXE SEDAN IS PARTLY
VIEW IN THE B.G.

PAN AWAY FROM HEART PUTTING
LDREN IN FRAME LEFT AS SNOOPY
TERS FRAME RIGHT. HE HAS
TATIC LOOK ON HIS FACE AS HE
RLY FLOATS IN, SMALL HEARTS
MATING OVER HIS HAND.

HE APPROACHES THE CAR, ROLLING
CK ON HIS HEELS.

HE DOES A HEADSTAND, ROLLS BACK
HIS FEET AGAIN ...

... AND KISSES THE CAR ON THE
NDER JUST BESIDE THE "FALCON
RIPT."

...THEN EXITS AS HE CAME. THE
MERA PANS BACK TO CENTER LINUS,
ARLIE BROWN AND PIG PEN. CAR IN
. CHARLIE SPEAKS HIS LINE LEAVING
NUS AND PIG PEN WITH A LOOK OF
RPRISE.

CLOSER SHOT OF ALL THREE
ILDREN.

AUDIO

LINUS:

Look Charlie Brown - it says here, "everyone loves the Ford Falcon". Do you really
think they mean everyone?

MUSIC: VERY LIGH , HEARTS AND FLOWERS-
TYPE THEME.

MUSIC: CONTINUES

MUSIC: CONTINUES

MUSIC AND EFFECTS: MUSIC IS PUNCTUATED
WITH SOUND EFFECT OF KISS THEN CONTINUES
AND FADES AS SNOOPY LEAVES.

CHARLIE:

Yes ... everyone!

ANNOUNCER:

Well it should be no surprise ... after
all the Falcon gives you so much more to
love than any other compact car.

LINUS:

That's very significant. Psychiatrists,
you know continually stress the importance
of love.

This is the script and storyboard for the first *Peanuts* Ford Falcon TV commercial, 1960, and represents the first time the *Peanuts* characters were ever animated for television. They appeared in black and white, and were animated by Bill Melendez, who would go on to work with Schulz on the landmark *A Charlie Brown Christmas* in 1965.

FORD WELCOMES CHARLIE BROWN

In this rough composite for a 1960 brochure announcing Ford's use of the *Peanuts* characters, the cast of the strip is introduced, followed by their creator.

I'VE HEARD OF WORKING FOR PEANUTS - BUT THIS IS A SWITCH!

HE'S ALREADY FEELING FORD'S NEW SALES FORCE...

I'LL HAVE TO TAKE OVER

*Charlie Brown and his gang of "Peanuts" fame ~ (Sparky Schulz's United Features Cartoon Feature with an audience of 9,000,000) have just signed up to sell the Ford line!

I WON'T EVER LET DOWN THE TEAM

INTRODUCING THE ONE AND ONLY
Charlie Brown

I LOVE BIRDS ESPECIALLY THOSE NAMED AFTER AUTOMOBILES

Li
HE'S SPEC

I ALMOST FORGOT THE MAN WHO MAKES US ALL POSSIBLE!

Charles "Sparkey" Schulz

A family man with ~~six~~ five children

As eccentric as these ceramic figures appear, they are also officially licensed *Peanuts* products made in Italy in 1969, hand painted and produced by Determined Productions. Left to right: Charlie Brown, Lucy, and Sally.

That night I sneak through abandoned trenches.

"Someday I'll get you, Red Baron!"

Snoopy's nemesis, the Red Baron, was never actually seen in the strip, but that didn't stop the Schmid company from producing this Red Baron music box as a companion to its Snoopy version of the same. When you turn the propeller, it plays "Auf Wiedersehen." 1972.

Opposite page: Psychiatrist Lucy treats Charlie Brown on this rare *Peanuts* music box from 1968, made in Italy by Anri. It plays "Try to Remember." This page: On another piece by the same company, Schroeder plays Beethoven's "Emperor" Concerto No. 5.

A rare *Peanuts* working toy piano, from the late 1960s, manufactured by T. J. Ely Mfg. Co.

Ceramic figure of Snoopy,
made in Italy in 1969 by
Determined Productions.

?

ZOOM!

ZOOM!

AAUGH!

3-17 **YOU DRIVE ME CRAZY!**

SCHULZ

HOW ARE YOU TODAY, SALLY?

I'M MAD! I'M MAD AT THE WHOLE WORLD!

ARE YOU MAD AT EVERYBODY IN THE WHOLE WORLD?

I'M MAD AT EVERYBODY!

ARE YOU MAD AT ALL THE ANIMALS AND THE BIRDS AND THE FISH?

HOW ABOUT ALL THE TREES AND ALL THE FLOWERS?

I'M MAD AT THEM, TOO! I'M MAD AT EVERYTHING!

ARE YOU MAD AT THE SKY? AND THE STARS? ARE YOU MAD AT THE GROUND? ARE YOU MAD AT ALL THE ROCKS?

ARE YOU MAD AT CARS AND BUILDINGS AND T.V. AND CIRCUSES AND ROLLER SKATES AND BRACELETS?

YOU DIDN'T MENTION JUMP ROPES...

OH, ARE YOU MAD AT JUMP ROPES, TOO?

I'M ESPECIALLY MAD AT STUPID JUMP ROPES!

SCHULZ

Comic book covers for Dell, early 1960s.

Undated sketch from the
mid-1950s of Lucy "wrist-
wrestling" Charlie Brown..

DELL

NO. 878
10¢

PEANUTS

ALL BRAND-NEW STORIES

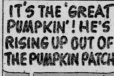

Linus's unwavering faith in the Great Pumpkin got its ultimate test when He finally "appeared" in 1961. How did this come about in the first place? "I can't remember exactly." said Schulz in 1967, "I know I was drawing some Halloween strips about Linus, who is bright but very innocent, and he was confusing Halloween with Christmas because he was one holiday ahead of himself. The whole thing became a parody of Christmas, and Linus gave the Great Pumpkin those qualities Santa Claus is supposed to have."

LINUS
OF THE PEANUTS COMIC STRIP

One of the delights of *Peanuts* is its total unpredictability. "I don't think it's necessary for every reader to understand every strip that you draw," Schulz said in 1981. Above: in a wonderfully bizarre idea from 1965, Lucy doesn't understand . . . until she does.

In an introduction to the first *Peanuts* book in Italian, the writer Umberto Eco said: "The poetry of these children is born from the fact that we find in them all the problems, all the sufferings of the adults, who remain offstage. These children affect us because in a certain sense they are monsters: they are the monstrous infantile reductions of all the neuroses of a modern citizen of the industrial civilization."

When asked his impression of this analysis in 1985, Schulz chuckled and said, "I think that's wonderful, that he should be able to say that. But it scares me, because I'm afraid somebody's going to say 'That's' all nonsense.' I think anybody who can write that well and thinks that much of my strip—that's really frightening."

"Charlie Brown's personality goes in several directions. Most of the time he is quite depressed because of the feelings of other people about him, but at the same time he has a certain amount of arrogance. Generally, however, he is wholly struck down by the re-marks of the other characters, especially Lucy. She represents all of the cold-blooded, self-sufficient people in this world who do not feel that it is at all necessary ever to say anything kind about anyone."
—from Schulz's *Developing a Comic Strip*, 1959

PEANUTS

YOU AND SNOOPY MUST BE TIRED AND HUNGRY FROM YOUR LONG WALK..

BEFORE YOU START TO TELL ME ABOUT THE "GREAT PUMPKIN," I'LL GET US SOME MILK TO DRINK

10-22

LAP! SLURP! LAP! SLURP! LAP! LAP!

Tm. Reg. U. S. Pat. Off.—All rights reserved
©1966 by United Feature Syndicate, Inc.

I GUESS I'VE SAID THIS BEFORE, BUT HE'S JUST ABOUT THE MOST PECULIAR KID I'VE EVER SEEN!

Schulz

PEANUTS

IF YOU HAVE SOME PROBLEM IN YOUR LIFE, DO YOU BELIEVE YOU SHOULD TRY TO SOLVE IT RIGHT AWAY OR THINK ABOUT IT FOR AWHILE?

4-15

OH, THINK ABOUT IT...BY ALL MEANS... I BELIEVE YOU SHOULD THINK ABOUT IT FOR AWHILE...

TO GIVE YOURSELF TIME TO DO THE RIGHT THING ABOUT THE PROBLEM?

NO, TO GIVE IT TIME TO GO AWAY!

Schulz

PEANUTS

CHARLIE BROWN, HOW DOES IT FEEL TO KNOW THAT YOU WILL NEVER BE A HERO?

WHAT MAKES YOU THINK I'LL NEVER BE A HERO? I MAY SURPRISE YOU! I MAY SAVE A LIFE OR REPORT A FIRE OR DO ALMOST ANYTHING!

LET ME PUT IT THIS WAY... HOW DOES IT FEEL WAY DOWN DEEP INSIDE IN YOUR VERY HEART OF HEARTS TO KNOW THAT YOU WILL NEVER BE A HERO?

1-3

TERRIBLE!

Schulz

PEANUTS

HEY, MANAGER, I CAN'T DO TWENTY PUSHUPS...

WELL, MAYBE YOU SHOULD START WITH JUST FIFTEEN OR MAYBE TEN...LET ME DEMONSTRATE...

PUSHUPS CAN BE VERY DIFFICULT IF YOU'RE OUT OF SHAPE..SOMETIMES IT'S BEST TO START WITH JUST...

...ONE!

Schulz   3-6

STEREO

COLUMBIA RECORDS

CS 8543

THE INCOMPARABLE COMIC STRIP COMES TO LIFE

PEANUTS

KAYE BALLARD AND ARTHUR SIEGEL?

COMPOSED AND CONDUCTED BY FRED KARLIN!

Kaye Ballard, of "The Mothers-in-Law" fame, recorded the first *Peanuts* record album for Columbia in the early 1960s.

Selchow and Richtor Co. made the first game featuring all the *Peanuts* characters in 1967.

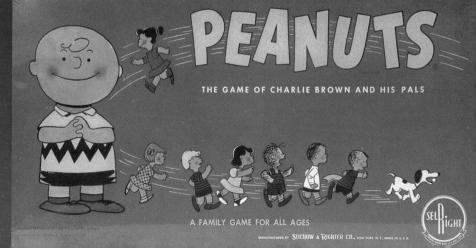

PEANUTS

THE GAME OF CHARLIE BROWN AND HIS PALS

A FAMILY GAME FOR ALL AGES

MANUFACTURED BY SELCHOW & RIGHTER CO., NEW YORK, N.Y. MADE IN U.S.A.

LINUS! YOU'RE NOT LEAVING, TOO?!

OF COURSE, I'M LEAVING! YOU CAN'T HAVE BASEBALL PRACTICE IN THE **RAIN**!!

AND DON'T TELL ME IT'S GONNA CLEAR UP BECAUSE IT ISN'T!!!

YOU'RE LOSING YOUR MIND, CHARLIE BROWN, THAT'S WHAT'S HAPPENING TO **YOU**!

ANYONE WHO HAS GOT SENSE ENOUG[H] GET IN OUT OF THE IS **CRAZY**!

YOU'RE A FANATIC, AND YOU'RE LOSING YOUR MIND!!

IT'S RAINING HARDER EVERY MINUTE, AND YOU WANT TO STAND OUT HERE, AND PLAY **BASEBALL**!

WELL, I SAY YOU'RE CRAZY, CHARLIE BROWN! I SAY...

CHARLIE BROWN?

CHARLIE BROWN?

4-3

HE SHOULDN'T LEFT...IT LOOKS IT MAY CLEAR U[P]

Tm. Reg. U. S. Pat Off.—All rights reserved
Copr. 1960 by United Feature Syndicate, Inc.

"PIG-PEN", YOU'RE A DISGRACE!

NO GIRL COULD EVER LIKE ANYONE AS DIRTY AS YOU!

GIRLS LIKE BOYS WHO ARE CLEAN AND NEAT AND WHO KEEP THEIR SHOELACES TIED!

BUT THERE ARE A LOT OF THINGS MORE IMPORTANT THAN JUST BEING CLEAN!

Tm. Reg. U. S. Pat Off.—All rights reserved
Copr. 1961 by United Feature Syndicate, Inc.

SOMEHOW, I NEVER QUITE KNOW WHAT'S GOING ON...

Non-sequiturs always made for great comedy. Charlie Brown uttered this punchline (left) a *lot*.

2-18

AAUGH! SOB

POOR SNOOPY...I SEE HE'S LOST ANOTHER FRIEND.. IT'S TOO BAD.... HE'S SO SENSITIVE...

UH, HUH... BUT I NOTICE HE WASN'T TOO SENSITIVE TO EAT THE CARROT!

To Jerry + Nora with friendship — Charles Schulz

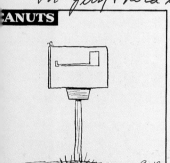

PEANUTS

OH, EXCUSE ME..

THAT'S ALL RIGHT... I'M EXPECTING WORD FROM MY PUBLISHER...

9-10

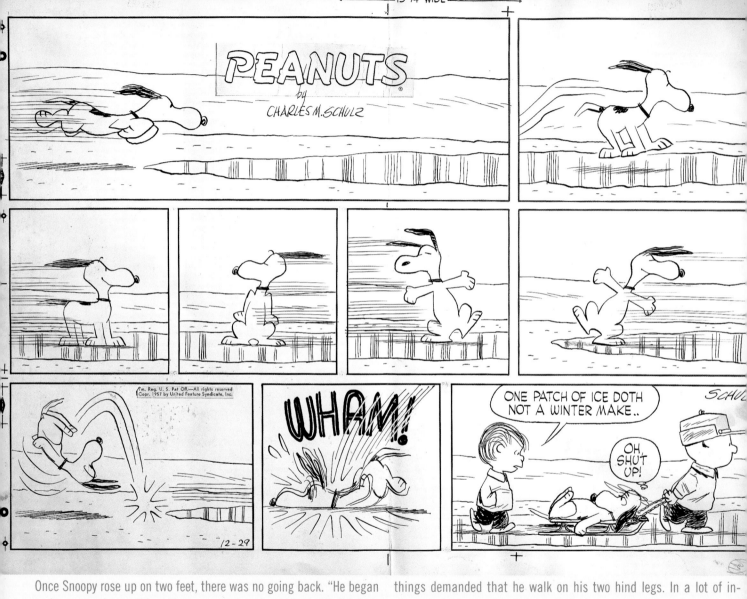

Once Snoopy rose up on two feet, there was no going back. "He began to do more and more things that were more and more fantastic," Schulz said in 1977, "it just seemed funnier at times to get him up. Some things demanded that he walk on his two hind legs. In a lot of instances, once you commit yourself that way you can't back up. It would be too late to put him back on four feet now. It would just destroy him."

The Hungerford Plastics Snoopy doll, 1958.

Right: The first Snoopy game, Selchow and Richtor Co., 1967.

Charlie Brown often found himself in the frustrating position of being constantly ridiculed by Snoopy even as he did his best to take care of him—something any parent could identify with.

The idea that Snoopy rarely referred to Charlie Brown by name, but almost always as "That round-headed kid," only added insult to injury.

Right: A Charlie Brown "Pocket Doll," from 1968. H. Boucher and Company also produced Snoopy (as the Red Baron), Lucy, Linus and Schroeder.

WELL, THOSE CLOUDS UP THERE LOOK TO ME LIKE THE MAP OF THE BRITISH HONDURAS ON THE CARIBBEAN..

THAT CLOUD UP THERE LOOKS A LITTLE LIKE THE PROFILE OF THOMAS EAKINS, THE FAMOUS PAINTER AND SCULPTOR...

8-14
UH HUH...THAT'S VERY GOOD... WHAT DO **YOU** SEE IN THE CLOUDS, CHARLIE BROWN?

PEANUTS 5-20

Tm. Reg. U.S. Pat. Off.—All rights reserved
© 1968 by United Feature Syndicate, Inc.

CHOMP!
CHOMP!
CHOMP!

I'M GOING TO BE VERY, VERY, VE
VERY, VERY, VERY, VERY SIC

276 - 350

PEANUTS

WHEN I'M REAL LONESOME, I LIKE TO GO TO MY DAD'S BARBER SHOP..

HE ALWAYS SMILES WHEN I GO IN, AND SAYS, "HI"

THE TWO MEN WHO WORK WITH HIM ARE NICE TO ME, TOO..

THEY ALWAYS ASK ME IF I'VE COME IN FOR A SHAVE

9-19

PEANUTS

BEFORE YOU SIT DOWN, WILL YOU GET ME A GLASS OF MILK?

I'VE ALREADY SAT DOWN

BEFORE YOU GET COMFORTABLE, WILL YOU GET ME A GLASS OF MILK?

I HAD SAT DOWN, BUT I HADN'T GOTTEN COMFORTABLE

SCHULZ

Schulz was a voracious reader. Among his favorite authors were Leo Tolstoy, Fyodor Dostoevsky, F. Scott Fitzgerald, Thomas Wolfe, Flannery O'Connor, Carson McCullers, Anne Tyler, and Joan Didion, just to name a few. *War and Peace* was his favorite novel, and his characters read and discussed it in dozens of strips. The reference to Edgar Allan Poe (opposite, top) is typical of the strip's many literary allusions.

 ...AND SO I CAN'T HELP IT.. I FEEL LONELY.. DEPRESSED...

 THIS IS RIDICULOUS!

 YOU SHOULD BE ASHAMED OF YOURSELF, CHARLIE BROWN!

YOU'VE GOT THE WHOLE WORLD TO LIVE IN! THERE'S BEAUTY ALL AROUND YOU! THERE ARE THINGS TO DO... GREAT THINGS TO BE ACCOMPLISHED!

 AN TRODS THIS EARTH ALONE! WE ARE TOGETHER; ONE GENERATION TAKING UP RE THE OTHER GENERATION HAS LEFT OFF!

 YOU'RE RIGHT, LUCY! YOU'RE RIGHT! YOU'VE MADE ME SEE THINGS DIFFERENTLY...

 I REALIZE NOW THAT I AM PART OF THIS WORLD... I AM NOT ALONE... I HAVE FRIENDS!

 NAME ONE!

 PSYCHIATRIC HELP 5¢ — THE DOCTOR IS IN — I'M IN SAD SHAPE!

 MY LIFE IS FULL OF FEAR AND ANXIETY.. THE ONLY THING THAT KEEPS ME GOING IS THIS BLANKET...I NEED HELP!

 WELL, AS THEY SAY ON T.V., THE MERE FACT THAT YOU REALIZE YOU NEED HELP, INDICATES THAT YOU ARE NOT TOO FAR GONE...

 I THINK WE HAD BETTER TRY TO PINPOINT YOUR FEARS...IF WE CAN FIND OUT WHAT IT IS YOU'RE AFRAID OF, WE CAN LABEL IT...

 ARE YOU AFRAID OF RESPONSIBILITY? IF YOU ARE, THEN YOU HAVE HYPENGYOPHOBIA!

 I DON'T THINK THAT'S QUITE IT.. HOW ABOUT CATS? IF YOU'RE AFRAID OF CATS, YOU HAVE AILUROPHOBIA

 WELL, SORT OF.. BUT I'M NOT SURE... ARE YOU AFRAID OF STAIRCASES? IF YOU ARE, THEN YOU HAVE CLIMACOPHOBIA

 MAYBE YOU HAVE THALASSOPHOBIA.. THIS IS A FEAR OF THE OCEAN, OR GEPHYROPHOBIA, WHICH IS A FEAR OF CROSSING BRIDGES...

 OR MAYBE YOU HAVE PANTOPHOBIA.. DO YOU THINK YOU MIGHT HAVE PANTOPHOBIA?

 WHAT'S PANTOPHOBIA? THE FEAR OF EVERYTHING..

 THAT'S IT!!!

This rare music box was made in Italy by Anri in 1969,

PEANUTS

PSYCHIATRIC HELP 5¢

NOW, YOU LISTEN TO ME, YOU STUPID BEAGLE..

THE DOCTOR IS IN

YOU CAME TO ME FOR HE AND YOU'RE GOING TO GE

WE'RE GOING TO HAVE A GOOD DOCTOR-PATIENT RELATIONSHIP, OR I'M GOING TO SLUG YOU! DO YOU UNDERSTAND?

THE DOCTOR IS IN

IT'S NOT NECESSA TO SALUTE...

THE DOCTOR IS IN

Lucy's psychiatric booth is one of Schulz's most brilliantly conceived creations. For someone who never actually went to a psychiatrist, his insight into their thought processes and methods was uncanny. Lucy's attitude about the entire enterprise could probably be best summed up by this exchange with Franklin from 1968, as he encountered her for the first time:

Franklin: "How's the lemonade business?"

Lucy: "This isn't a lemonade stand . . . this is a psychiatric booth."

Franklin: "Are you a real doctor?"

Lucy: "Was the lemonade ever any good?"

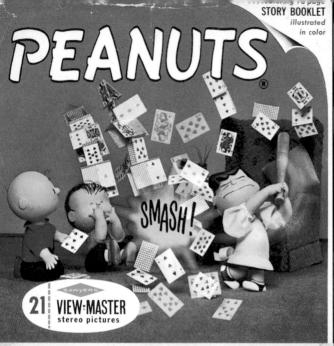

View-Master Reels combine the beauty of color with the realism of stereo to make pictures "Come to Life."

Each Packet contains three 7-scene Reels — or twenty-one full-color three-dimension pictures.

The Wonderful World of PEANUTS

▸ STORY DESCRIPTIONS ▸

View-Master Reel One

GOOD GRIEF, BEETHOVEN!

When music pours from Schroeder's tiny piano, it melts even the heart of Lucy. But when she put her portrait on the piano in place of Beethoven's bust . . . . !!!

View-Master Reel Two

STEAAAADY! CHARLIE BROWN

Out of the fresh, pure, goodness of his heart, Charlie Brown (who never seems to learn) showed Linus how to build a house of cards.

View-Master Reel Three

THROW IT HOME, SNOOPY!

Charlie Brown spends many lonely hours on pitcher's mound. This time Pig-Pen walloped the ball and Snoopy made a miraculous save . . . and "loneliness" was not the word for what happened next!

A **16-page color illustrated booklet** ALSO INCLUDED

In 1966 View-Master created a series of tableaux based on *Peanuts* strips, to be seen through one of their trademark stereoptic viewers. Translating Schulz's drawings into three dimensions is no easy task, but these offer a charming take on what the characters could look like in the "real world."

"Snoopy's not a real dog, of course—he's an image of what people would like a dog to be."

—1967

Opposite and overleaf:
From sketches to finishes, Snoopy at the typewriter, late 1960s.

"MMMMMM!"

MMMMM!

"It's exciting when you've written something that you know is good!"

IT'S EXCITING WHEN YOU'VE WRITTEN SOMETHING THAT YOU KNOW IS GOOD!

Joe Anthro was an authority on Egyptian and Babylonian culture. His greatest accomplishment, however, was his famous work on the Throat culture.

It was a dark and stormy night

Suddenly a shot rang out. A door slammed. The maid screamed. Suddenly a pirate ship appeared on the horizon. While millions of people were starving, the king lived in luxury.

Meanwhile, on a small farm in

Kansas, a boy was growing up.
End of Part I

Part II
A light snow was falling, and the little girl with the tattered shawl had not sold a violet all day.

From *Newsday*, 1977:
Interviewer: "Snoopy writing at the typewriter, how did that start?"
Schulz: "It probably began with the dark and stormy night sequence. It might have been that I thought of that first and simply applied it to the dog writing at the typewriter. But since then I have done a lot of things with it and I have enjoyed it. Again, each theme that you think of seems to serve its purpose by giving you an outlet for all the ideas that come to you. Now some of the ideas for puns that Snoopy writes could never be used in the strip itself; they are simply too corny. But when Snoopy writes them, and writes them with all sincerity, then they are funny. You don't think that Snoopy is being stupid or anything like that. You like him for his naiveté because he innocently thinks he has done something great, and that makes it acceptable."

At that very moment, a young intern at City Hospital was making an important discovery.

I MAY HAVE WRITTEN MYSELF INTO A CORNER...

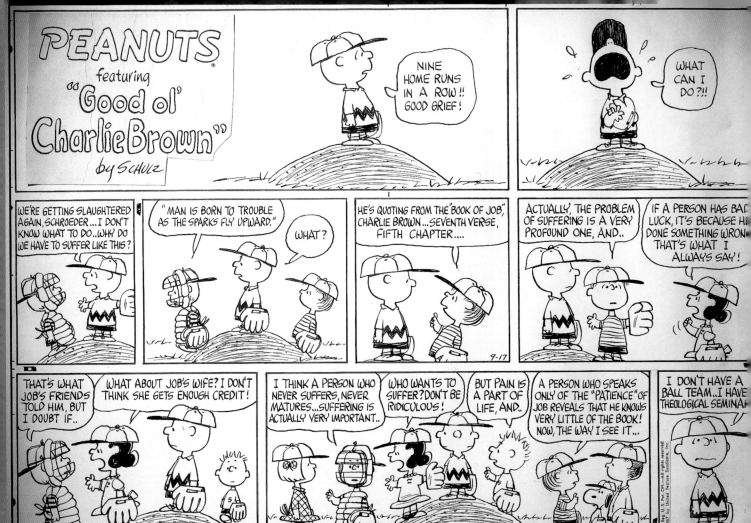

This unusual exchange took place in the *Los Angeles Times* in 1973:

Schulz: "Apparently Linus is a good [baseball] player and Schroeder is a good catcher. I think Charlie Brown's outfield is no good. He has the three girls out there. Lucy is obviously a bad player. But we've never found out, really, why they lose all those games. Charlie Brown looks as though he's pitching pretty well."

Interviewer: "You talk as if you're puzzled yourself."
Schulz: "Yeah. I really don't know why it is."
Interviewer: "Well, if you don't know, we're in trouble."
Schulz: "Yes, I suppose. You know, we don't even know who they're playing."

Whether or not Schulz is just having a little fun here is unclear, but he often spoke of the characters as if he had little or no control over them.

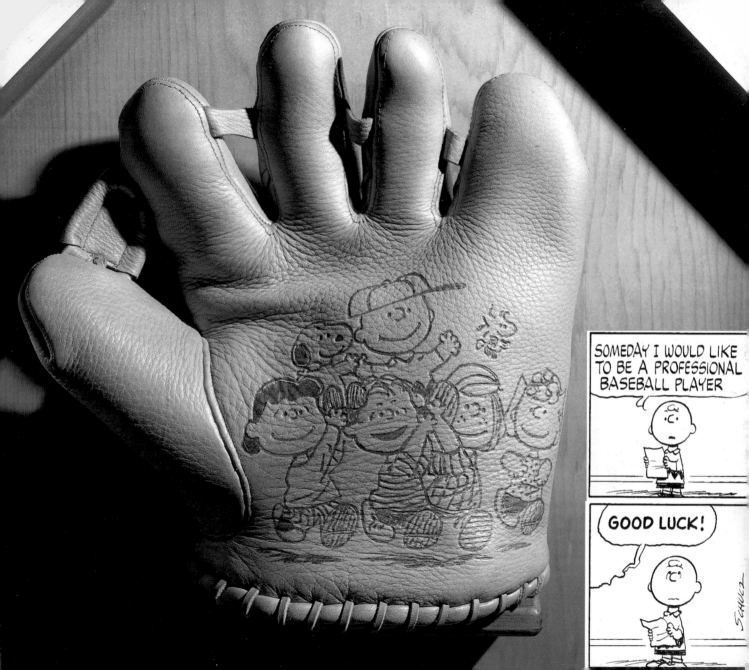

CHARLIE BROWN
OF THE PEANUTS COMIC STRIP

I NEED ALL THE FRIENDS I CAN GET

Schulz's working sketchbook for *I Need All the Friends I Can Get* affords a rare look at his thought process from initial drawings and text to the final form (above, and subsequent yellow pages). *Friends* is the 1964 follow-up title to the immensely popular *Happiness is a Warm Puppy* and *Security is a Thumb and a Blanket*, in which a single theme is explored—this time, Friendship.

What started out as a horizontal format ended up square, which when opened then became the extended rectangle. We present here the entire sketchbook, which contains material that didn't make the cut. Likewise, passages that are found in the printed book were not part of his initial ideas.

I NEED ALL
THE FRIENDS
I CAN GET

This sketchbook is from the private collection of Schulz's son Craig, who found it after the fire in 1966 that burned Schulz's Sebastopol (Ca.) studio to the ground. Schulz gave the book to a friend of Craig's named Dan Northern, who kept it for 25 years. When Northern came across it in the 1990s, he returned it to Craig. This is its first publication.

I NEED ALL THE FRIENDS I CAN GET

I NEED ALL THE FRIENDS I CAN GET

"WELL, I HATE TO SPOIL ALL THE FUN, BUT I HAVE TO BE GOING."

"Well, I hate to spoil all the fun, but I have to be going."

" I SAID I HATE TO SPOIL ALL THE FUN, BUT I HAVE TO BE GOING..."

"SIGH"

"NOBODY LIKES ME...NOBODY REALLY LIKES ME...
NOBODY CARES IF I LIVE OR DIE!"

"Nobody likes me . . .
Nobody cares if I live or die!"

"WHAT'S THE MATTER WITH YOU?"

"I DON'T HAVE ANY FRIENDS..."

"DEFINE 'FRIEND'..."

"OH, GOOD GRIEF!"

"hat's the matter with you?''

"THE TROUBLE WITH YOU, CHARLIE BROWN, IS YOU TRY TOO HARD!"

6

"NOW, TAKE ME, FOR INSTANCE... I DON'T TRY TO MAKE FRIENDS BECAUSE I REALLY DON'T NEED ANY FRIENDS! I'M SELF-SUFFICIENT!"

7

"Define 'Friend'!"

"WELL, I'M NOT... I NEED ALL THE FRIENDS I CAN GET!"

"WHAT DO YOU THINK A FRIEND IS,
PIG-PEN?"

"A "A FRIEND IS SOMEONE WHO ACCEPTS YOU
FOR WHAT YOU ARE"

" I ACCEPT YOU, OLD FRIEND......MORE OR LESS..."

"A friend
is someone
who accepts
you for what
you are."

This extended sequence with Snoopy and the birds was eventually cut, because it didn't fit the single panel format.

But it did appear in the regular daily strip, and Snoopy's little feathered pals would eventually evolve into Woodstock.

"A FRIEND IS **NOT** SOMEONE WHO TAKES ADVANTAGE OF YOU!"

I DON'T KNOW... I THINK I'D SETTLE FOR
EVEN A 'FAIR-WEATHER FRIEND!'"

"A friend
is someone
who's willing to
watch the program
you want to
watch!"

"A friend
is someone
who likes you
even when the
other guys are
around."

"A FRIEND IS SOMEONE WHO IS WILLING TO WATCH WHATEVER
YOU WANT TO WATCH"

"A FRIEND IS SOMEONE WHO LIKES YOU EVEN WHEN THE
OTHER GUYS ARE AROUND"

"A FRIEND IS SOMEONE YOU CAN TRUST WITH YOUR LIBRARY CARD!"

"A friend is someone who ll take the side with the sun in his eyes."

"A FRIEND IS SOMEONE WHO WILL TAKE THE SIDE WITH THE SUN IN HIS EYES"

"A FRIEND IS SOMEONE YOU CAN SOCK ON THE SHOULDER" *arm*

"A FRIEND IS SOMEONE YOU CAN CALL UP IN THE MIDDLE OF THE NIGHT"

"A FRIEND IS SOMEONE WHO LIKES YOU IN SPITE OF YOUR FAULTS"

"WELL, WHAT I MEAN IS, IF TWO PEOPLE, A BOY AND A GIRL, THAT IS... ARE FRIENDS, CAN'T THAT FRIENDSHIP GROW TO BE ... WELL, YOU KNOW WHAT I MEAN...."

"NO, I DON'T KNOW WHAT YOU MEAN"

"A friend is someone you have things in common with, Charlie Brown."

"A friend is someone who doesn't think it's crazy to collect old Henry Busse records!"

The sketchbook and the final version end very differently. In the former, Lucy grudgingly consoles Charlie Brown (even though he is a blockhead). In the latter, Linus offers his allegiance, with genuine feeling (below). The Gentle wins out over the Crabby yet again.

"I LIKE YOU, CHARLIE BROWN...EVEN THOUGH I KNOW YOU'RE A BLOCKHEAD!"

"All these definitions   "'Friend'...A person whom one   "That's me!"   "W

The Red Baron has been reported in the vicinity of Saint-Mihiel. I must bring him down. "Switch off!" cries my mechanic. "Coupez!" I reply. "Contact?" "Contact it is!"

DRAT THIS FOG! IT'S BAD NOUGH HAVING TO FIGHT THE RED FRON WITHOUT HAVING TO FLY IN FATHER LIKE THIS. WHEN I GET. BACK I'M GOING TO WRITE A LETTER TO PRESIDENT WILSON!

Snoopy's busy fantasy life emerged in the mid-1960s, as he assumed the mantle of a World War I flying ace, battling it out with his nemesis, the Red Baron. This surreal turn of events brought the strip into new, and newly delightful, territory by achieving a level of absurdity that seemed somehow perfectly normal. To Snoopy at least. "He has to retreat into his fanciful world in order to survive," said Schulz in 1997. "Otherwise, he leads kind of a dull, miserable life. I don't envy dogs the way they have to live."

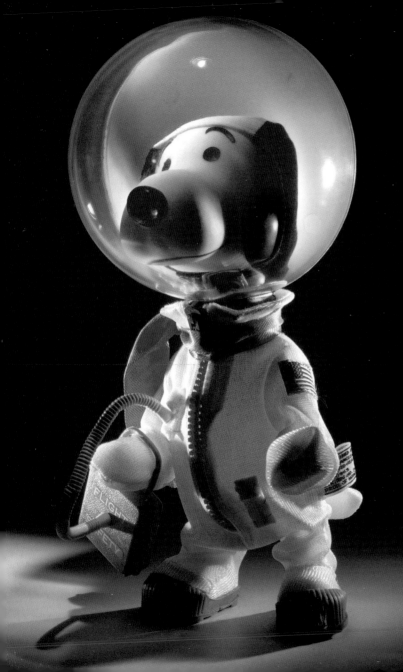

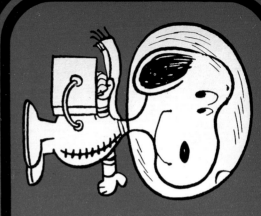

SNOOPY
ASTRONAUT

In 1969 the Apollo X space mission named their command module "Charlie Brown," and their lunar module "Snoopy." They didn't actually land on the moon, but the "real" Snoopy did.

Above: This 1969 Anri music box from Italy commemorating the event is extremely rare and plays the song "The Battle Hymn of the Republic."

Opposite: Determined Production's Snoopy Astronaut doll, 1969.

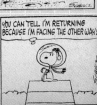

PEANUTS

HELLO, CHUCK? I NEED YOUR HELP.. I NEED SOMEONE TO TALK TO

GUESS WHAT HAPPENED...THEY WON'T LET ME WEAR MY SANDALS TO SCHOOL ANY MORE..IT'S AGAINST THE DRESS CODE...WHAT AM I GOING TO DO? I NEED YOUR ADVICE...

WELL, I...I...I DON'T KNOW...I... YOU...I...I...IT...YOU...I..I..I.....

THANKS, CHUCK.. click!

✳ SIGH ✳

PEANUTS

AN AQUARIUM? IT'S VERY NICE, BUT WHAT MADE YOU DECIDE TO BUY AN AQUARIUM?

IT'S TIMELY! HAVEN'T YOU HEARD? THIS IS THE AGE OF AQUARIUMS!

AQUARIUS

WHAT?

FORGET IT!

BIG BROTHERS NEVER KNOW WHAT THEY'RE TALKING ABOUT

PEANUTS

YOU'RE GOING TO WALK CLEAR ACROSS TOWN TO LEND SOMEONE YOUR BASEBALL GLOVE?

PEPPERMINT PATTY'S TEAM NEEDS IT

THEN WHY DON'T THEY ASK YOU TO PLAY?

THEY DON'T NEED ME..THEY NEED MY GLOVE

THEN LET HER COME AND GET IT HERSELF!

I'M JUST TRYING TO BE NICE

GOOD LUCK WITH THE WORLD!

PEANUTS

HERE I AM AT THE DAISY HILL PUPPY FARM ABOUT TO MAKE MY SPEECH..

AH, THE INTRODUCTION IS OVER... I'M ON!

✳ AHEM ✳

BONK!

?!

"I developed the character Peppermint Patty because I happened to be walking through our living room. I saw a dish of Peppermint Patties and I thought that would make a good name for a character, so I drew the face to match the name. One day I sent her to camp, and a little girl came into her tent one night and said, 'Sir, my stomach hurts.' That was Marcie."

PEANUTS

BIRDS HAVE SCARY DREAMS..

7½ 7 9½   NO SPS

PEANUTS Columbus Day by Sally Brown

THIS IS A REPORT FOR SCHOOL

I SEE

Columbus Day was a very brave man. He wanted to sail around the world.

"I can give you three ships, Mr. Day," said the Queen.

GOOD LUCK

THANK YOU

7½ — 9½

PEANUTS WOODSTOCK IS THE ONLY BIRD I KNOW WHO CAN'T FIND HIS OWN WAY SOUTH..

OH, WELL, I DON'T REALLY HAVE ANYTHING ELSE TO DO, AND I'M SORT OF ENJOYING THE TRIP

HE'S NOT AN EASY PERSON TO TRAVEL WITH, THOUGH...

FOR ONE THING, HE HATES TO EAT AT A PLACE WHERE YOU HAVE TO SIT AT A COUNTER..

PEANUTS I'M WRITING A STORY ABOUT SOME CAVE MEN

THEY'RE SITTING AROUND A CAMP FIRE, SEE, WHEN ALL OF A SUDDEN THEY'RE ATTACKED BY A HUGE THESAURUS!

VOLUME ONE OR VOLUME TWO?

IT'S IMPOSSIBLE TO DISCUSS ANYTHING WITH A BIG BROTHER!

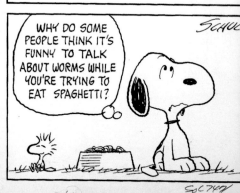

"Cartooning really is just designing," Schulz said in 1997. "It's a lot like Picasso on paintings. Take the shape of Charlie Brown's head . . . If a cartooning style is too extreme, the artist can never do or say anything that is at all sensitive. If you look back upon all of the great comic strips down through the years, every one of them was drawn in a style that was relatively quiet." By way of example, some of Schulz's favorite strips were *Krazy Kat, Skippy,* and *Gasoline Alley.*

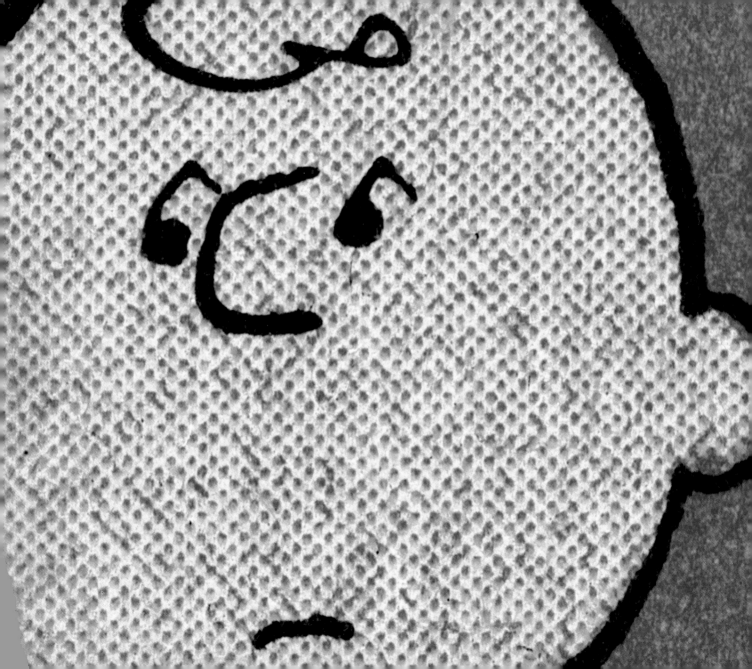

PEANUTS

RAIN! GOOD GRIEF!

HOW CAN YOU HAVE FUN AT CAMP WITH DORKY WEATHER LIKE THIS? I WONDER HOW CHUCK IS DOING?

SIR, WHAT TIME IS LUNCH?

DON'T CALL ME "SIR"! WHAT KIND OF A DORKY KID ARE YOU?

DORKY?

7-20

PEANUTS

WELL, SNOOPY, HERE WE ARE AT CAMP...

MUST BE AN ARTILLERY OUTFIT.. I FEEL SORRY FOR THE POOR BLIGHTERS WHO HAVE TO LIVE HERE

I SUPPOSE THE FIRST THING TO DO IS TO MEET OUR TENTMATE

HI, THERE... MY NAME IS CHARLIE BROWN.. I GUESS WE..

SHUT UP AND LEAVE ME ALONE!

PEANUTS

HEY, LOOK... I GOT A LETTER FROM THAT KID I MET AT CAMP

WE WERE TENTMATES... I WROTE TO HIM, BUT I GUESS I REALLY DIDN'T THINK HE'D ANSWER...HOW ABOUT THAT?

8-23

WHAT DOES HE SAY?

"SHUT UP, AND LEAVE ME ALONE!"

PEANUTS

HELLO, SCHROEDER?

NOW THAT YOU AND I ARE THROUGH, WHY DO YOU KEEP CALLING ME ON THE PHONE?

9-15

I DIDN'T CALL YOU... YOU CALLED ME!

HOW COME YOU NEVER GET A WRONG NUMBER WHEN YOU NEED ONE?

KNOCK KNOCK

NOW THAT YOU AND I ARE THROUGH, SCHROEDER, I'M RETURNING ALL THE GIFTS I WAS GOING TO GIVE YOU...

THANK YOU

THAT DIDN'T EVEN MAKE SENSE!

I JUST GOT BACK FROM THE SHOW..

THE MAN THERE SAID THAT HIS THEATER COST TWO MILLION DOLLARS...

HE SAID HE DIDN'T MIND THOUGH BECAUSE HE WAS GOING TO CHARGE ME TWO MILLION DOLLARS FOR MY TICKET, AND THAT WAY HE'D GET IT ALL BACK AT ONE TIME...

I THINK HE WAS TEASING ME

THERE HE IS! THERE'S CHUCK! WHERE'S HE GOING?

IT LOOKS LIKE HE'S GOING HOME, SIR.

STOP CALLING ME "SIR"! HEY, CHUCK, WHAT'S THE MATTER? WHAT ABOUT OUR GAME?

I'LL BET HE HEARD WHAT YOU SAID ABOUT HIM, SIR...ABOUT HOW HE'S DULL AND WISHY-WASHY AND THAT NO ONE COULD EVER BE IN LOVE WITH HIM...

CHUCK! COME BACK! I DIDN'T MEAN IT! I DIDN'T KNOW YOU WERE LISTENING! CHUCK!!

HA HA, HERMAN.. *SIGH*

TOMORROW NIGHT IS OUR BIG NIGHT, LINUS..

ALL YOU HAVE TO DO IS WALK UP TO A HOUSE, RING THE DOORBELL AND SAY, "TRICKS OR TREATS!"

ARE YOU SURE THAT'S LEGAL?

OF COURSE, IT'S LEGAL!

GOOD... I WOULDN'T WANT TO BE ACCUSED OF TAKING PART IN A RUMBLE!

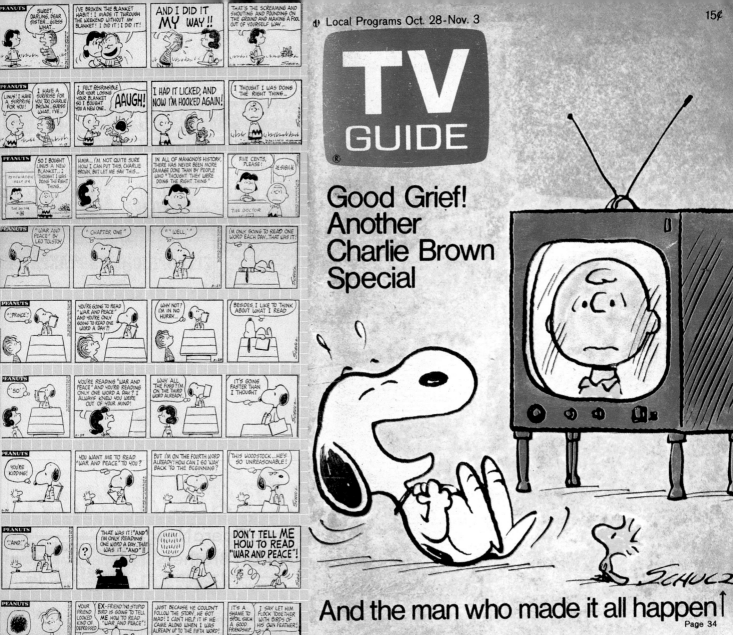

Local Programs Oct. 28 - Nov. 3

15¢

TV GUIDE ®

Good Grief! Another Charlie Brown Special

And the man who made it all happen↑

Page 34

PEANUTS

Dear Santa Claus, Do you need a secretary to help during the holiday season?

I could answer letters and run errands, and I will work for only five-hundred dollars a week.

FIVE HUNDRED DOLLARS A WEEK?!

WHY NOT? EVERYONE KNOWS THE OLD GUY IS LOADED!

11-30

PEANUTS

THE GROUND IS COVERED WITH SNOW..WE SHOULD THROW SOME BREAD OUT FOR THE BIRDS...

THAT'S A GOOD IDEA..

BONK!

12-2

PEANUTS

OKAY, YOU STUPID BEAGLE, LET'S GET AT IT AGAIN..

THIS MORNING WE'LL WORK ON OUR DUTCH WALTZ...WE START IN THE "KILIAN" POSITION...

THE MAN'S HAND IS FIRMLY ON THE HIP OF HIS PARTNER, AND THE GIRL PRESSES HER HAND FIRMLY ON HIS...

HOW COZY!

WE'RE GOING TO BE THE BEST ACT IN THE SHOW..

STICK WITH ME, SWEETIE, AND YOU'LL GO PLACES!

12-11

PEANUTS

WAKE UP, YOU STUPID BEAGLE, IT'S FIVE O'CLOCK!

OH, NO!

IF WE'RE GOING TO SKATE IN THE CHRISTMAS SHOW, WE'VE GOT TO PRACTICE AND PRACTICE AND PRACTICE!

WHILE THE STARS ARE STILL OUT?

STOP COMPLAINING... GETTING UP EARLY IN THE MORNING IS GOOD FOR YOU...

I **HOPE** IT'S GOOD FOR ME BECAUSE IT'S KILLING ME!

12-13

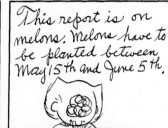

"I think the Little League setup is deplorable," said Schulz in 1973. "First, the players are judged by age. Age has almost nothing to do with evaluating or placing players. If there's a 12-year-old kid who stands 6 feet and can throw the ball so fast the other kids can't see it, he shouldn't be allowed to dominate the game. He should be pushed up to a higher league, where he fits in."

13¾" WIDE   No SRS

PEANUTS® featuring "Good ol' Charlie Brown" by Schulz

STRIKE TWO!

STRIKE THREE!

RATS!

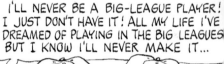

I'LL NEVER BE A BIG-LEAGUE PLAYER! I JUST DON'T HAVE IT! ALL MY LIFE I'VE DREAMED OF PLAYING IN THE BIG LEAGUES BUT I KNOW I'LL NEVER MAKE IT...

YOU'RE THINKING TOO FAR AHEAD, CHARLIE BROWN...WHAT YOU NEED TO DO IS TO SET YOURSELF MORE IMMEDIATE GOALS...

IMMEDIATE GOALS?   YES

START WITH THIS NEXT INNING WHEN YOU GO OUT TO PITCH...

SEE IF YOU CAN WALK OUT TO THE MOUND WITHOUT FALLING DOWN!

7-2

Nor did he share the American obsession with winning. "No sooner does the season start than we begin to record how far a team is out of first place. A game between two teams in 7th and 10th place can be just as exciting as any game. But all we're worrying about is who wins. It should be the plays, great goals being scored, great baskets being made, great overhand shots hit. These are the things that count in sports."

PEANUTS

IS THIS YOUR BEACH BALL?

HEY! YEAH! THANK YOU VERY MUCH!

I WAS SWIMMING OUT THERE, AND IT CAME FLOATING BY..

MY SILLY SISTER THREW IT INTO THE WATER

I SEE YOU'RE MAKING A SAND CASTLE..

IT LOOKS KIND OF CROOKED

I GUESS MAYBE IT IS.. WHERE I COME FROM, I'M NOT FAMOUS FOR DOING THINGS RIGHT...

PEANUTS

IS YOUR WHOLE FAMILY HERE AT THE BEACH, FRANKLIN?

NO, MY DAD IS OVER IN VIETNAM

MY DAD'S A BARBER. HE WAS IN A WAR, TOO, BUT I DON'T KNOW WHICH ONE

DO YOU LIKE BASEBALL, CHARLIE BROWN?

MY PROBLEM IS I LIKE BASEBALL TOO MUCH

ARE YOU A GOOD PLAYER?

I HAVE SOME FRIENDS WHO WOULD REGARD THAT AS A GREAT TOPIC FOR A PANEL DISCUSSION

Franklin, the strip's first African-American, debuted in 1968. Not meant as a comment on any specific facet of urban culture, he was just a *Peanuts* character who happened to be black. Even at that time, it was a problem for some. "I got a letter from one southern editor," Schulz remembered in 1997, "who said something about 'I don't mind you having a black character, but please don't show them in school together.' Because I had shown Franklin sitting in front of Peppermint Patty. I didn't even answer him."

PEANUTS

WE ALL NEED HOPE, FRANKLIN, DID YOU KNOW THAT?

AND WE ALL NEED MEMORIES... WITHOUT GOOD MEMORIES, LIFE CAN BE PRETTY SKUNGIE...

I HAD THREE GOOD MEMORIES ONCE...

BUT I FORGOT WHAT THEY WERE!

PEANUTS

HOW ABOUT A GAME OF MARBLES AFTER SCHOOL, FRANKLIN?

I CAN'T..I HAVE A GUITAR LESSON AT THREE-THIRTY...

RIGHT AFTER THAT I HAVE LITTLE LEAGUE, AND THEN SWIM CLUB, AND THEN DINNER AND THEN A '4 H' MEETING

I LEAD A VERY ACTIVE TUESDAY!

PEANUTS

..FAMILY.. THIS "WAR AND PEACE" IS A GREAT BOOK..

A CAT'S GOT WOODSTOCK!

THE CAT NEXT DOOR HAS GOT WOODSTOCK! SAVE HIM! SAVE HIM!! GOOD GRIEF!

ROWRR!!

PEANUTS

I APOLOGIZE, SNOOPY..

I THOUGHT THE CAT NEXT DOOR HAD GOTTEN WOODSTOCK, BUT IT WAS ONLY AN OLD YELLOW GLOVE...

BUT IT PROVED ONE THING, DIDN'T IT? IT PROVED YOU WERE WILLING TO GIVE YOUR LIFE FOR YOUR FRIEND! YOU COULD HAVE BEEN KILLED!

YOU THINK I'M ALIVE?

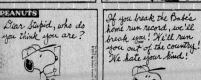

Peanuts team rosters, over the years:
Pitcher/Manager: Charlie Brown, Catcher: Schroeder, First Base: Shermy, Second Base: Linus (and Pig-Pen, at least once), Third base: Pig-Pen (and Violet, at least once), Shortstop: Snoopy (also a sometime outfielder), Left Field: Patty (and Rerun, once), Center Field: Frieda (and Violet or Lucy, on occasion), Right Field: Lucy.

PEANUTS
featuring
"Good ol' Charlie Brown"
by Schulz

Madam Fullcharge

I'M READY!

SO IT'S "SHOW AND TELL" TIME AGAIN, IS IT? WELL, DO I EVER HAVE A SURPRISE FOR YOU TODAY!

I HAVE A LITTLE FILM TO SHOW YOU THAT'S GONNA KNOCK YOUR EYES OUT!

NO, MA'AM... THAT'S ONLY AN EXPRESSION..

1-20

ALL RIGHT, IF I CAN HAVE A COUPLE OF YOU STRONG TYPES LIFT THIS PROJECTOR INTO PLACE, WE CAN GET THIS SHOW ON THE ROAD!

NO, LET'S PUT IT ON THAT TABLE BACK THERE... HOW ABOUT YOU FOUR WEIRDOS MOVING THAT TABLE?

AND I'LL NEED A COUPLE MORE TO PUT THIS SCREEN U LET'S GO!! ON TH DOUBLE, THERE!

STRETCH THAT CORD ACROSS THE BACK, AND PLUG IT INTO THAT SOCKET IN THE CORNER...

OKAY, SOMEONE RUN DOWN TO THE CUSTODIAN THEN, AND GET AN EXTENSION! YOU THERE, GET GOING!!

NOW, WHAT ABOUT THOSE WINDOW SHADES? LET'S HAVE ALL OF YOU WHO SIT ALONG THE SIDE THERE PULL DOWN THOSE STUPID SHADES..

AND I'LL NEED SOMEONE ON THE LIGHT SWITCH... ONE VOLUNTEER... YOU THERE, HONEY, GET THE SWITCH!

IS THAT THE BELL ALREADY?

OKAY, WE'LL TAKE IT TOMORROW FROM HERE EVERYONE BE IN PLACE B NINE! THANK YOU, AND GOOD MORNING!

Sally's travails at school provided hilarious material, and her presentations to the class became a *Peanuts* staple, starting in 1970. A few excerpts from her "reports," delivered with the utmost authority: "Abraham Lincoln was our sixteenth king, and the father of Lot's wife." (2/12/70); "The largest dinosaur that ever lived was the Bronchitis. It soon became extinct . . . it coughed a lot." (12/11/72);

"Butterflies are free. What does this mean? It means you can have all of them you want." (5/4/73); "This is my report on rain. Rain is water which does not come out of faucets . . . after a storm, the rain goes down the drain, which is where I sometimes feel my education is also going." (11/7/73); "Light travels at a speed of 186,000 miles per second . . . so why are afternoons so long?" (6/1/76)

In 1973 Sally brought Snoopy in for Show and Tell and lived to regret it.

This is yet another example at how good Schulz was when it came to the characters "acting."

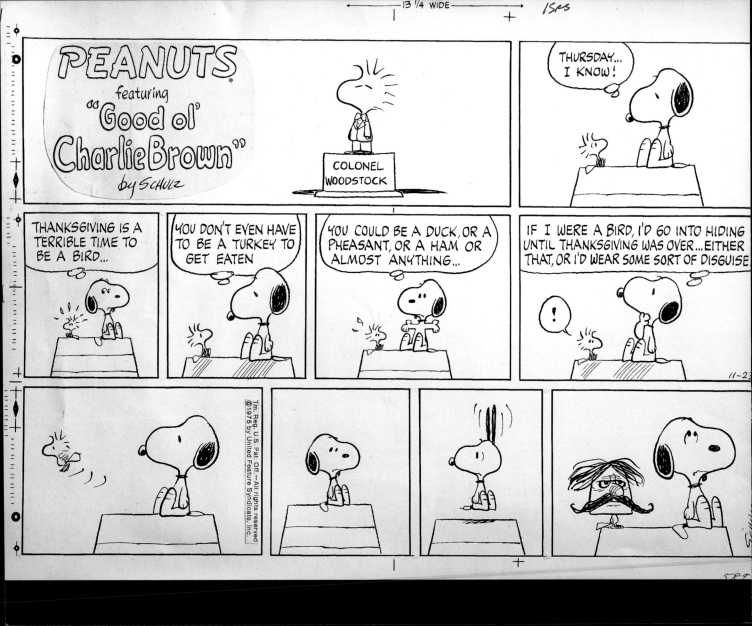

PEANUTS featuring "Good ol' Charlie Brown" by SCHULZ

I'LL NEVER GO SWIMMING IN THE OCEAN AGAIN!

?

WOW!

PAWPET THEATER

TEETH

NOW PLAYING EXCITING! TERRIFYING!

11-30

WHAT'S SO TERRIFYING ABOUT **THIS** SHOW?

I DON'T SEE ANYTHING VERY EXCITING, EITHER!

I THOUGHT THIS WAS SUPPOSED TO BE A SCARY SHOW...

WHEN DO WE GET TO THE SCARY PART?

YOU NEVER HAVE ANY SELF-DOUBTS, DO YOU?

ME?

HAHAHAHA!!

NO, I GUESS NOT

11-28

SLAM

THAT STUPID CHARLIE BROWN! HE HAD THE NERVE TO SAY THAT I'M NOT PERFECT!

SO I SUPPOSE YOU HIT HIM, HUH?

RATS! I KNEW I FORGOT SOMETHING!

11-30

A NEW YEAR'S TOAST!

12-30

TO THAT WONDERFUL GENIUS...

TO THAT PERSON WE ALL ADMIRE...

THE INVENTOR OF THE DOGGIE BAG!

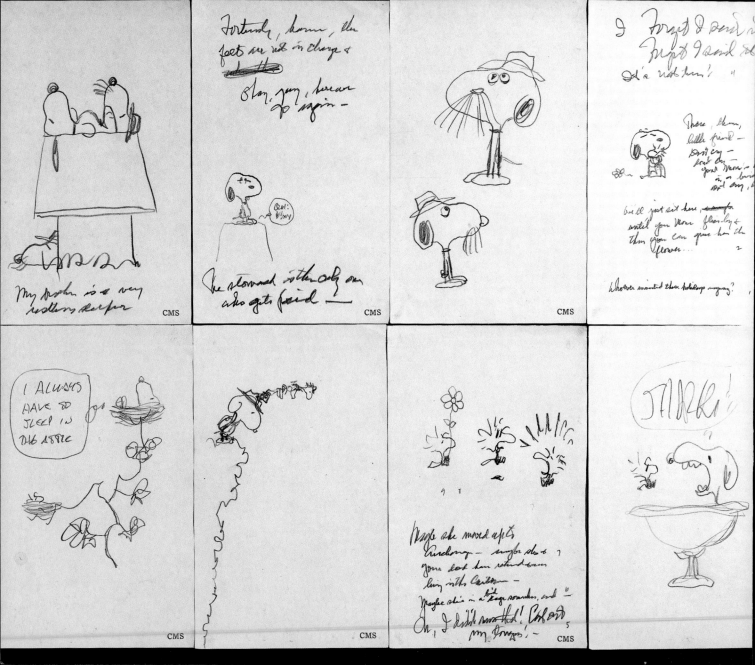

TODAY IS OUR LAST DAY OF SCHOOL

DOES ANYONE WANT TO KNOW WHEN CHARLES DICKENS WAS BORN?

OR HOW HIGH MOUNT WHITNEY IS? OR HOW TO SPELL MISSISSIPPI?

ASK ME IN SEPTEMBER!

BONK!

DID IT EVER OCCUR TO YOU THAT YOU MIGHT BE FACING THE WRONG WAY?!

BONK!

WHY DO WE ALWAYS TEACH LITTLE KIDS TO WAVE "BYE-BYE"?

BECAUSE FOR THE REST OF HIS LIFE PEOPLE WILL BE LEAVING HIM

HELLO, THERE!

ERASE SCRUB ERASE
ERASE SCRUB ERASE
ERASE SCRUB ERASE

WHOOPS! NOW I'VE DONE IT!

WHAT HAPPENED, SIR?

I ERASED MY WHOLE DESK!

DO YOU KNOW WHAT TOMORROW IS, SIR?

I CAN'T IMAGINE

TOMORROW IS THE FIRST DAY OF SCHOOL

Z

"How can we lose when we're so sincere?"

—CHARLIE BROWN, 1963

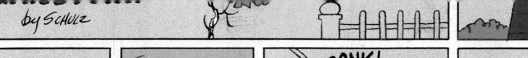

BONK!

LAWYERS DON'T INTIMIDATE ME!

From a 1985 *International Herald Tribune* interview:
Interviewer: "What character has changed the most in your eye?"
Schulz: "Snoopy! Snoopy started off as simply a cute little dog, a cute little puppy and then he grew to a very grossly caricatured those days. If the syndicate had any sense, they would have called me up and said, 'You're fired, we hate the way you're drawing.' But I have to keep going back to warmth. There was harshness to some of the things that I was drawing at a certain

THE OTHER DAY I SAW THIS KID AND A DOG PLAYING A GAME.. THE KID THREW A STICK AND THE DOG WOULD CHASE IT..

THAT WOULD BE NICE

Dear Santa Claus, I saw a recent picture of you in a magazine.

12-3

You look fatter than ever.

I know how you usually fly through the air with your reindeer and sleigh.

© 1985 United Feature Syndicate, Inc.

I'll be surprised this year if you even get off the ground.

Schulz

HEY, KID..DID YOU EVER THINK ABOUT SANTA CLAUS HAVING A CORONARY?

A WHAT?

12-11

See SANTA Today- Hours 1-3

WHEN YOU GET UP THERE TO TALK TO HIM, CHECK HIS EAR LOBES...

DO WHAT?

A DEEP CREASE IN THE EAR LOBES COULD INDICATE CHANGE IN CORONARY VESSELS...

© 1985 United Feature Syndicate, Inc.

CHECK HIS EAR LOBES..

DO WHAT?!

Schulz

In 1987, the Peanuts logo changed, from the original hand lettering to this new machine font.

PEANUTS®

by

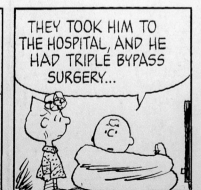

PEANUTS

by Schulz

I REALLY NEED YOUR HELP...

BUT I'M NO GOOD AT THIS KIND OF THING

PEOPLE HAVE TO KNOW ABOUT THE "GREAT PUMPKIN"...

YOU'LL BE DOING THEM A REAL SERVICE, CHARLIE BROWN..

I'LL TAKE THAT SIDE OF THE STREET, AND YOU TAKE THIS SIDE...

BUT IT'S SO EMBARRASSING..

10-28

RING!

GOOD MORNING! I'M HERE TO TELL YOU ABOUT THE "GREAT PUMPKIN"

ON HALLOWEEN NIGHT THE "GREAT PUMPKIN" RISES OUT OF THE PUMPKIN PATCH AND BRINGS TOYS TO ALL THE CHILDREN IN THE WORLD!

I DID IT!

BUT I'M SURE GLAD NO ONE ANSWERED THE DOOR!

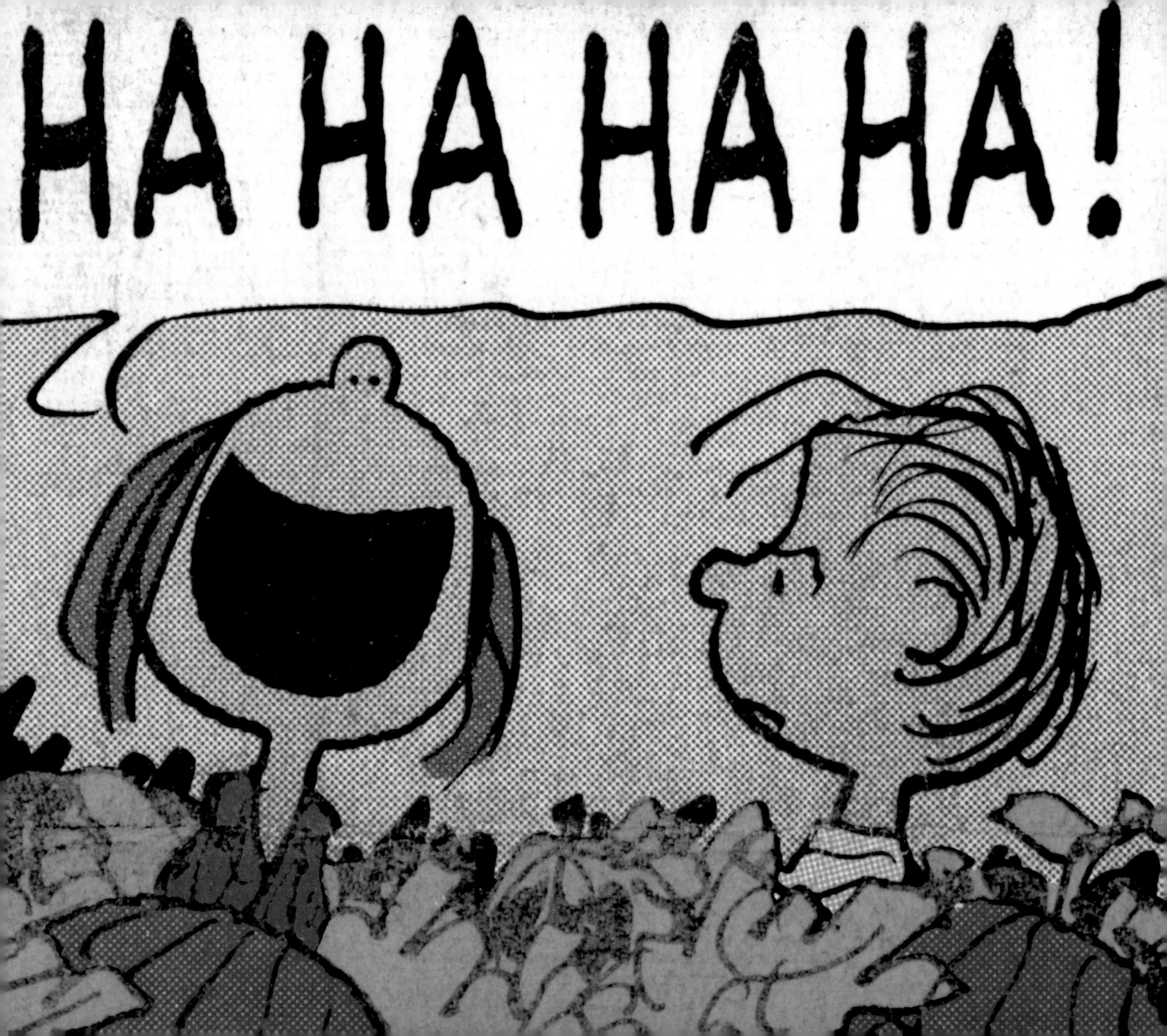
HA HA HA HA HA HA!

I SPEND HALF MY LIFE STANDING AROUND WAITING FOR HIM..

THIS HAPPENS EVERY TIME WE GO FOR A WALK...

HE ALWAYS HAS TO STOP AND LOOK THROUGH ALL THE OUT-OF-TOWN PAPERS..

I KNOW THE ANSWER! IT WAS HENRY VEE!

HENRY VEE WAS KING OF ENGLAND IN 1413!

10-15

HENRY V, SIR... NOT HENRY VEE..

© 1985 United Feature Syndicate, Inc.

AND ANOTHER PUPIL SINKS SLOWLY BENEATH HER DESK...

HALLEY'S COMET IS ACTUALLY A LARGE CHUNK OF DIRTY ICE...

THE NEXT TIME IT PASSES OUR EARTH WILL BE IN THE YEAR 2062...

10-18

OF COURSE, WE'LL ALL BE EIGHTY YEARS OLD WHEN THAT HAPPENS...

EXCEPT FOR YOU, MA'AM..

© 1985 United Feature Syndicate, Inc.

From the *Dayton Daily News and Herald Magazine*; May 3, 1987:
Interviewer: "The drawing [by now] must be getting easier."
Schulz: "Except for my hand shaking. I have a problem and I don't know if it has been since the heart surgery, but I have to draw much more slowly. I'm not as facile as I used to be."

Rather than harming the strip, this actually made the linework even more expressive, and marked the further evolution of *Peanuts* through the 1980s and 90s. Due to Schulz's discipline and mastery of technique, the gradually wavier lines never looked like a mistake—they were a natural, effective design choice.

Panel 1: THIS PROGRAM IS CALLED "GREAT IDEAS OF WESTERN MAN"

© 1985 United Feature Syndicate, Inc.

Panel 2: WHY DON'T YOU GET UP OUT OF THAT BEANBAG, AND LET ME LIE THERE?

10-19

Panel 3: NOW, WHY DON'T YOU GO INTO THE KITCHEN, AND GET ME A DISH OF ICE CREAM?

Panel 4: " GREAT IDEAS OF WESTERN WOMAN!"

Panel 5: HERE'S THE "LONE BEAGLE" MAKING HIS HISTORIC FLIGHT ACROSS THE ATLANTIC TO PARIS...

22

Panel 6: FAR BELOW HE CAN SEE THE DARK WATERS OF THE ATLANTIC...

© 1985 United Feature Syndicate, Inc.

Panel 7: YOUR WATER DISH IS GETTING LOW.. I THINK I'D BETTER FILL IT...

Panel 8: THE DARK WATERS OF THE ATLANTIC DISAPPEAR BENEATH HIS PLANE...

Panel 9: THIS IS YOUR REPORTER INTERVIEWING THE FAMOUS "LONE BEAGLE" AFTER HIS FLIGHT ACROSS THE ATLANTIC

Panel 10: HOW DID YOU FEEL AFTER YOU LANDED? HOW DID YOU FEEL WHEN YOU TOOK OFF? HOW DO YOU FEEL?

10-24

Panel 11: IF YOU WERE A TREE, WHAT KIND OF TREE WOULD YOU LIKE TO BE? HOW DOES IT FEEL TO HAVE FEELINGS? HOW DO YOU FEEL?

Panel 12: * boot! BACK TO OUR STUDIO!

© 1985 United Feature Syndicate, Inc.

...
TS
SURE WE DO...I'VE ALWAYS REGRETTED THAT I COULDN'T GROW A BEARD...
SCHULZ
© 1985 United Feature Syndicate, Inc.

From Schulz's keynote speech to the National Cartoonists' Society convention, 1994:

"I am still searching for that wonderful pen line that comes down when you are drawing Linus standing there, and you start with the pen up near the back of his neck, and you bring it down and bring it out, and the pen point fans a little bit, and you come down here and draw the lines this way for the marks on his sweater. This is what it's all about—to get feelings of depth and roundness, and the pen line is the best pen line you can make. That's what it's all about."

MAY

10	11	12	13	14	15	16
17	18	19	20	21	22	23
24	25	26	27	28	29	30
31	1	2	3	4	5	6

"All you're trying to do is fill in those squares. Do something good for Monday, and then do something good for Tuesday, and then you do something for Wednesday. Where does it all come from?"

—C. M. SCHULZ, 1997

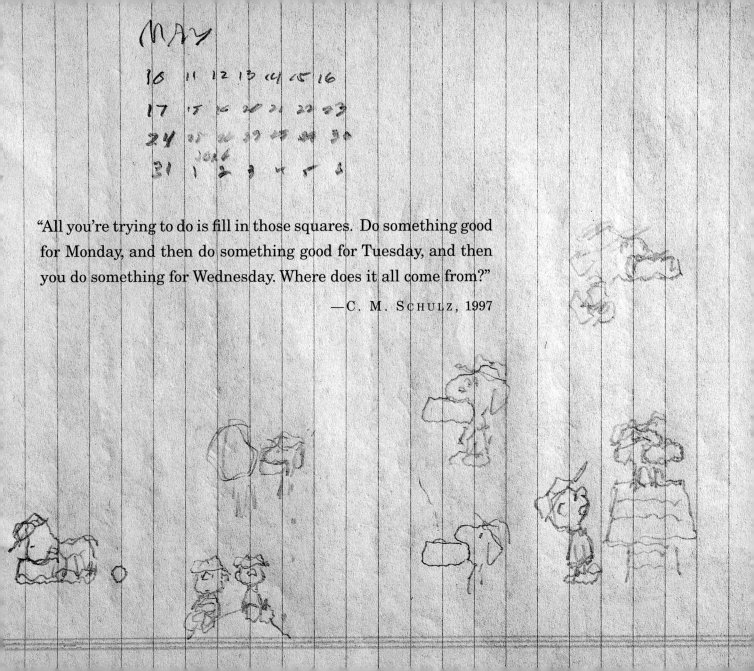

Constructing a storyline for the week: "Monday- he gets a bicycle. But what happens on Tuesday?" sketches from 1999.

No, I don't
think anyone
comes out here
anymore

"She really can't help herself," Schulz wrote of Lucy and the football, in 1985. "She is annoyed that it's all too easy. Charlie Brown isn't that much of a challenge. To be consistent, however, we have to let her triumph, for all the loves in the strip are unrequited; all the baseball games are lost; all the test scores are D-minuses; the Great Pumpkin never comes; and the football is always pulled away."

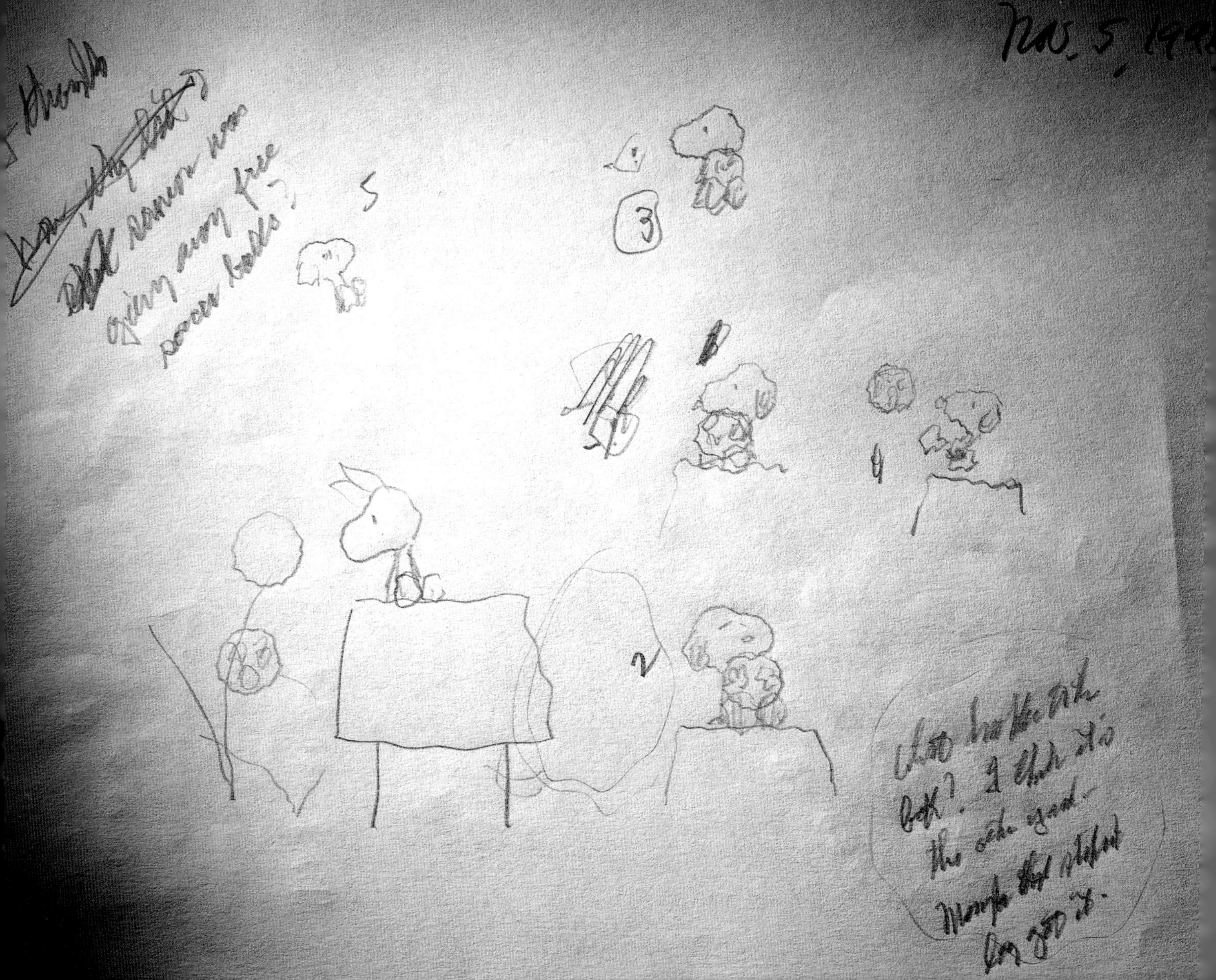

sible without her. Likewise Paige Braddock and all the staff at Creative Associates in Santa Rosa, Ca. Monte and Craig Schulz graciously allowed us into their homes to photograph memorabilia and artwork, which was invaluable.

If the attention to detail of the line quality, paper texture, and ink dots in this book made your eyes water, that's because of Geoff Spear's brilliant photographs. He, like Peppermint Patty, is a rare gem.

Chris Ware lent us his extraordinary collection of vintage *Peanuts* strips, as well as encouragement and a keen eye.

At Pantheon: Shelley Wanger steered this book through its complicated evolution with grace and patience. Andy Hughes handled production with his trademark mastery, along with Altie Karper, Serena Park, and Ann Lin.

At United Media: Thanks to Jennifer Buchanan, Janine Hallisey, Amy Lago, and

Jean Sagendorph. Their trust in this book helped us see it through.

John Kuramoto's assistance in Santa Rosa was crucial, Seth provided obscure facts and ephemera, and the intrepid Freddi Margolin schlepped her wonderful toys into my office all the way from Long Island. Also thanks to Nat Gertler, David Michaelis, Patrick McDonnell, Gary Groth, John Keene, Ivan Brunetti, J. D. McClatchy, and Dan Clowes. Special thanks to Roberta "Bobbie" Miller.

All quotes from Charles Schulz were cited from the book *Charles M. Schulz: Conversations* (University Press of Mississippi, 2000, M. Thomas Inge, ed.) unless otherwise indicated—many, many, thanks to all of the interviewers.　　—C. K.

COLOPHON

All of the drawings in this book were photographed from the originals or from strips clipped from the newspaper when they first appeared, using a Linhof 4" x 5" camera. Two hundred and five shots were taken, comprising over 1,025 exposures.

The typefaces are **Trade Gothic** (sans serif) and **Century Schoolbook** (serif). Both were staples of 20th-century American newspaper composition.

The layout was assembled in Quark Express 4.1

Opposite: Unfinished lettering and sketches found next to Schulz's desk, July 2000.

11-13-98